PRINCESS OF ELM

Warriors of the Fianna
Book Four

by
Sophia Nye

ARE YOU SIGNED UP FOR DRAGONBLADE'S BLOG?

You'll get the latest news and information on exclusive giveaways, exclusive excerpts, coming releases, sales, free books, cover reveals and more.

Check out our complete list of authors, too!

No spam, no junk. That's a promise!

Sign Up Here

www.dragonbladepublishing.com

Dearest Reader;

Thank you for your support of a small press. At Dragonblade Publishing, we strive to bring you the highest quality Historical Romance from some of the best authors in the business. Without your support, there is no 'us', so we sincerely hope you adore these stories and find some new favorite authors along the way.

Happy Reading!

CEO, Dragonblade Publishing

Additional Dragonblade Books by Author Sophia Nye

Warriors of the Fianna Series
Song of the Fianna (Book 1)
Prince of Fire (Book 2)
Into the Ashes (Book 3)
Princess of Elm (Book 4)

Also from Sophia Nye
Outlawed (Novella)

The Warriors of the Fianna

Deep in the heart of the Kingdom of Munster, the legendary King Brian Boru has brought an ancient brotherhood back to life: The Fianna. Now entering his senescence, King Brian has all but achieved his dream of becoming High King of Éire, uniting the nine kingdoms to defend Éire's emerald shores from *Fin Gall* raiders. He will need the aid of the kingdom's best warriors to complete his vision and claim the seat of the High King.

But it is no simple task to become a warrior of the Fianna. Seven trials, the same seven used by the ancient Fianna, test the mettle of all who would claim such an honor.

Intelligence: Memorize the twelve books of poetry, so that you may be knowledgeable on the history, genealogy, and legends of your people.

Defense: With naught but staff and shield, defend yourself from nine men's spears while standing deep in a hole.

Speed: Outrun pursuers through a forest, without being injured. But take care! Not a branch may be broken to prove your skill.

Movement: Leap over a tree with a height to match your own, then crawl beneath a branch lower than your knee.

Recovery: Run through the forest with all speed until you step upon a thorn. Remove it without slowing down!

Bravery: Fight outnumbered without faltering.

Chivalry: Marry for love.

Truth in our hearts,

Strength in our arms,

Honesty in our speech.

PROLOGUE

Caiseal, Éire
Spring, 986

"Hurry up," Cormac hissed at his younger brothers, knowing he'd be the one in trouble if they were caught. The reprieve of warm spring weather beckoned, and the three brothers answered her call. They'd had enough of spending the beautiful, warm sunshine-filled days trapped inside attending their lessons. Even intermittent drizzles didn't dampen their desire to get out and explore.

"Let's go," Conan hurried along young Diarmid. At eight years old, Diarmid struggled to keep up with his older brothers.

Today, they decided they'd waited long enough to have a bit of fun, especially since tomorrow their family arrived. Their elder sister, Dunla, would marry King Brian Boru of Mumhain, the man under whom they now fostered. Cormac remembered some of his earliest years at home, but he'd been living in Caiseal with Brian since his seventh summer, as was the tradition. The memories he had of his family, his parents, his elder sister and brother, and even his younger siblings who fostered here with him, were a mixture of emotions and snippets, nothing tangible he could recall aside from their father's ill temper.

The boys ran through the wooded hillsides of the fortress at Caiseal, having easily slipped past the guards and out the gate. They had but one goal in mind: Freedom.

"I think we should go swim in the river," Diarmid declared,

huffing and puffing as he followed behind his two older brothers.

"I want to catch a frog," Conan replied.

"That's bad luck," Diarmid shot back, squishing his small nose in disapproval.

Cormac just listened, leading them onwards and praying they didn't get caught. Spring brought magic to the woods, filling it with the calls of birds they hadn't heard in months. Leaves high and low shone a bright golden green as they awakened from winter's slumber.

In spite of the promise of a new year, Cormac couldn't quite shake a feeling of dread that bubbled up at the thought of seeing his family again. He knew his brothers looked forward to seeing their parents, but after spending seven years at home and seven years with Brian, Cormac determined that his parents were not the sort who enjoyed the company of children. And, though he was a child no longer, he couldn't forget their poor temperaments and harsh discipline. Even as a young man, he didn't relish the thought of returning to that sort of place.

A gentle breeze rustled the fresh leaves on the trees as they ran. Everything glistened after a morning of soft rain. Cormac struggled to keep his footing as they forded the trees and hills and giant roots that filled the undulating hillsides.

At the river, a slow, bubbling spring fed into shallow, crystalline waters. Diarmid's shoes flew off the moment they sighted the spring, and Cormac had to shout at him to make sure he took the rest of his clothes off, too. That way he didn't ruin either the clothes or their chances of sneaking back in without Brian realizing where they'd gone. Diarmid dutifully obeyed, the gleeful grin on his face never faltering.

As he jumped into the river and splashed about, Conan, the middle child, watched Diarmid splashing with a frown. Cormac realized Conan would never find frogs or turtles or even fish with Diarmid dancing about and making such a racket.

Instead, Cormac suggested that they build a small shelter, a hideout where they could come and play anytime they were able to sneak away from their lessons this summer. The pair of them worked the rest of the afternoon, piling stones and fallen logs into a shape that resembled something akin to a small home, though nowhere near as grand as the hall at Caiseal.

"Don't you think it's a bit odd that Dunla's marrying Brian?" Conan asked as he placed a stone that was probably too large for a boy his size. Conan had always been strong for his age.

"I think it's fabulous!" Diarmid shouted, still splashing wildly in the water. "I'm so glad they're coming back."

"You know they're leaving again in another week or two. They're only staying for a short while," Conan told him.

Diarmid continued as thought Conan hadn't spoken. "It's been forever since I've seen them."

"It's been a year since you've seen them," Cormac corrected him with a small smile. He'd always envied Diarmid's exuberance, his ability to embrace everything life threw at him with joy and optimism. "And I do think it's a little odd," he added, answering Conan's earlier question. "But she's a lot older than us, and kings always marry young ladies who have many years left to give them sons."

"But he's already got sons," Diarmid called, tossing water high above his head so that it glittered in the sunshine as it cascaded down about him.

"And he's got us," Conan added, puffing up his chest proudly. "I'll be such a good foster son that he won't even need that baby."

"Why did he keep him anyway? Diarmid asked. "Shouldn't the baby have gone with his mother when she left?"

They spoke of Brian's recent separation from his third wife, Gormla. Cormac didn't know what had transpired between Gormla and Brian. He'd observed that their tempers clashed more than they didn't, and it only worsened after the birth of their son, Duncan, a year ago. They divorced months ago and Gormla returned to live with her older son and daughter in Dyflin, along Éire's eastern shore.

"He's keeping Duncan because he asked her to leave him. He

asked for him to stay," Conan explained calmly to his younger brother.

"He asked for him to stay because he loves children," Cormac added thoughtfully.

Both his brothers nodded their approval at his answer, as though that settled the matter.

They spent much of the afternoon in hot debate over the impending arrival of their family, their siblings, and the unusual situation of their sister marrying their foster father. By the time they hiked back up through the wooded hillside, their stomachs grumbled in hungry protest at the day's exertions. It seemed they'd have to wait a bit longer for dinner, though.

When they reached the gate to Brian's keep, Osgar, the king's manservant, stood with his arms crossed and a great frown on his heavily browed face.

"I was told to keep an eye out for you three," he said sternly, looking from one boy to the next. "Brian wants to see you in his solar."

"God's bones," Diarmid muttered under his breath. Cormac smacked him on the arm, reminding him to mind his mouth. They were already in enough trouble.

The boys found Brian waiting before a crackling fire, even in the warm, sunny afternoon. Brian had fires more often than not of late, compared with Cormac's earlier years of fosterage. Though he was only of middling years, his reddish-brown hair had already gone mostly grey, but he still looked every inch the tall, formidable warrior, just as mighty now as in his youth. Or so Cormac imagined.

The moment they entered the room, Brian looked up from his seat by the fire, locking eyes with Cormac and beginning a speech that Cormac was certain would not end well for them. A knot formed in the pit of his stomach as he prepared for the tongue lashing they'd earned.

"Do you know why your namesake, the great King Cormac, the legend from ancient times, wrote that every high king should have a druid as one of his advisors? And why we also keep priests and monks, all of them near to us? Why we protect them?"

Cormac stopped himself from tossing a wild guess at his foster father, instead shaking his head.

"It's because they are the wise, the ones who have learned more than most men. And because they will make the best decisions." He paused, letting his words sink in as the three boys squirmed with guilt at skipping out on their lessons. "I know it can be difficult, to sit for so long and to study so hard when you haven't cause to use any of it, but you will. You are all princes. Any of you could rule your father's kingdom in the years to come.

"If you are not learned, then you will surely be foolish. I will not send back fools to your father in place of princes. Now, as the weather warms, perhaps we can work out an arrangement where you can have short trips out to explore the woodlands, for that is also a useful skill. And we can increase your training time, but only if you continue with your lessons at the same pace. It will be more work, but it will also give you more freedom. Is that an acceptable solution?"

"Yes, lord," Cormac answered hurriedly, setting the example for his brothers as he always tried to do. The other two quickly responded the same.

"I'm sorry, lord." Cormac apologized, looking to his brothers, who then did the same yet again. "We were wrong, and we will do better."

Brian nodded to them, and as they retreated to go find dinner at last, Cormac couldn't help but feel that he was lucky to have such a calm and reasonable foster father, one who truly had their best interests at heart.

That was the day Cormac always thought of as the last day of his childhood. It was the last time he was more interested in playing and chasing the joys of life than he was in any of the serious business that was the domain of men. For the following day, their family arrived from Connachta. And with them, came the end of his childhood.

The feasting hall was a sight to behold, a splendorous affair filled with flowers in vases and hanging from the rafters. Gilded cups adorned every seat and embroidered cloths covered the tables. Cormac couldn't remember there ever being a feast quite like this one in the halls of Caiseal. Despite his trepidation at the appearance of their parents, he looked forward to seeing his elder sister and brother again, and at the prospect of such a fine feast to come.

Cormac's father Cahill was one of a long line of kings of the Kingdom of Connachta, north of the Kingdom of Mumhain, where he and his brothers lived as foster children of Brian. Cormac's mother, Enat, also hailed from a prestigious family further to the north. Cormac didn't dislike them. Indeed, as any young son, he loved his parents and wanted only their approval. Until he came to live with Brian, that was.

The stark difference between Brian and his own father resonated with Cormac more and more as he grew into a man. Brian was the sort of man he wanted to become, not his cold, distant, and ill-tempered father.

When the family arrived, they asked for a private audience with their three sons. Cormac entered Brian's solar first, struck by how different his siblings looked since he'd seen them last. Teague had the same dark hair that all of them shared, but he kept his long and tied away from his face—that much had not changed. But his shoulders were broader than their father's, his face sharper, all traces of his childhood long gone. Beside him, Dunla, the eldest, could have been their mother twenty years earlier for they shared the same heart-shaped face, high cheekbones, and piercing blue eyes.

Diarmid rushed toward their mother, who pulled him into a rather short hug. He then tried to go hug their father, but Cahill placed his hands on his youngest son's shoulders, turned him around, and shoved him over toward his sister, who eagerly embraced her youngest brother. Dunla seemed more happy than nervous, surprising for a bride who was about to wed a man nearly twice her age. At least she'd met Brian before, but Cormac imagined that she'd never considered him as a potential husband. Cormac would speak to her later of her true feelings on the matter. "Well?" Cahill demanded of his sons. "How have you been? Are you treated well?"

"Aye, very well," Conan replied, shifting his feet anxiously.

Cormac didn't feel the need to speak just yet.

Several exchanges of niceties passed before their father asked for everyone but Cormac to leave the hall, dismissing his youngest children rather coolly considering the length of time they'd spent apart. Diarmid had been away only a year, but to a boy of eight it felt an eternity. Conan had been gone nearly as long as Cormac at his twelve years of age.

"As I'm certain you're aware, I expect you to return home with us after the wedding," Cahill announced.

Cormac had not been aware, but he nodded his understanding. A knot wrenched in the pit of his stomach like a fist squeezing his insides as he thought about leaving Caiseal—his home—behind.

"That's all." His father waved dismissively.

Cormac nodded again, taking his leave and finding his brothers to get started on their new studies, putting the conversation with his father from his mind.

THE FOLLOWING DAY was the wedding. Cormac remembered little of it, for the wedding was not the memorable part. It was the reception afterward that stuck in his mind like a thorn in his skin, digging deeper and deeper until it festered.

That evening started out as well as not. Dancing and merriment, the sounds of laughter and singing and music filled the night air under a glowing half moon. The night held a chill, but the proliferation of bodies and exuberant dancing kept Cormac too warm to wear his cloak. He stood on the fringe of the celebration, watching his two brothers dance happily with the first girls they could ensnare to do so. He shook his head as he watched them gleefully sweeping across the center of the courtyard. Bright colors, loud noises, and laughter were the things Cormac remembered most when he thought back on that night prior to the fight.

In the midst of the celebration, a commotion broke out. Shouting and clattering and then silence.

Cormac hurried along the edge, toward the shouting. He shoved his way through a ring of onlookers that had formed around the two kings, Brian and his father. His brothers appeared beside him moments later. All of them—Teague, Conan, and Diarmid—stood slack jawed, watching Brian and their father shout at one another, red-faced and furious.

"If we sit and do nothing, we'll lose the whole of the island, Cahill! The incursions of the Fin Gall have only worsened in the past years, and I tire of watching them drive their spike of death further into the heart of Éire. Malachy stands by and does nothing! You may not be willing to take a stand and fight, but I am, and others are as well."

His father shouted so angrily that Cormac could hardly make out the words, but he understood that his father strongly disagreed.

"I will not stay in the house of a traitor to the king," Cahill spat at the end of his tirade, enunciating each word through gritted teeth.

"If you will not take advantage of an opportunity for all the kingdoms to unite against a common enemy and cease this bickering amongst ourselves, then I cannot help you," Brian growled.

"I will not resort to blows at my daughter's wedding." Cahill's voice went eerily quiet. "But you and I, we are finished." He turned, finding his four sons—Teague, Cormac, Conan, and Diarmid. "Let's go. Now."

Teague did as he was told, walking to stand beside Cahill without hesitation.

Cormac's feet stood rooted to the ground beneath him. He agreed with Brian. The Fin Gall were raiding deeper and deeper inland. Entire villages had been massacred. And they were spreading and settling, setting up outposts so they could continue driving further toward the heart of the island. Brian was right. If they did nothing, then there would be nothing left. No place seemed safe from their raiding.

Cormac knew that his future, and even that of his brothers, would depend on his next move. They always did as he did, thinking him older and wiser. Clearly, they weren't privy to his thoughts, for if they saw his mind now they would know that he floundered like a landed fish.

This moment would be a turning point for the rest of his life. His dinner threatened to burst from his belly. The blood drained from his face, but he stood firm, shaking his head in the face of his father's anger.

"We stay," Cormac declared, "and we fight."

"Then you are no sons of mine," Cahill spat, turning on his heels and pulling their mother and Teague out with him.

Cormac's heart tore in two as he watched them walk away, wondering if his brothers would ever forgive him.

CHAPTER ONE

Dyflin, Éire
December, 1001

F RIGID WATERS BROKE upon the bow, sending a thousand icy
pinpricks against her face in a tempestuous spray of foamy
brine. The taste of salt permeated the air so fully that she could
breathe it in with every leap the longship took over the frothing
waves. *This* was the way life was meant to be lived: crashing
headlong through whatever waves the stormy sea demanded.

Astrid's eyes shut, her face upturned against the onslaught of
the voyage as she stood behind the prow of her brother's
longship. Their father had made a far longer journey, first to
Laithlinn and then, years later, to Éire. He left his own kingdom a
warrior, but he died in this new land a king. From her youth,
Astrid dreamed of visiting the land of her father, of living in a
place filled with her own people.

She felt her brother's approach, the sound of his steps echoing
off the oaken planks.

"You choose the strangest days to come out with us," Sitric
remarked. Even though he took up the mantle of kingship over
the harbor town at Dyflin after fighting hard for it, Astrid always
thought him too kind a soul for the position.

"It's colder than this in the lands of our ancestors." She
opened her eyes, taking in the tall figure of her brother. With his
long, golden hair and thick beard, he clearly took after their
father. "It's good practice."

"Astrid."

She hated the sympathy in his voice almost as much as she hated being separated from the rest of their kin. "I simply don't understand why we can't return. Leave all this nonsense with Brian and Laigin and all the hundreds of other kings behind our oars."

"The nonsense would follow us." He leaned against the prow, his gaze straying to the seething waters beyond. "The petty squabbles between kings drove Father away from his people. We would be trading one spider's web for another, and in leaving we would destroy the kingdom he spent his life building."

Her hands squeezed into fists, bringing back some of the feeling stolen by the cold. No matter how many times she broached this conversation, her brother threw platitudes and excuses at her. But she would not bend so easily.

"Then let me go alone," she tried, already knowing that Sitric would argue. "Stay here and uphold our family's future while I seek out its past."

"You know I cannot." His ice-blue eyes, the same color as the roiling winter sea, flashed to her. "I am responsible for your safety, a duty I cannot adequately perform whilst in a different kingdom."

"Do you never long to see it?" she pressed, growing desperate. "Do you never dream of seeing your true home?"

Sitric turned to her fully, his face too serious. Her brother rarely felt the weight of his responsibilities. Like their father, he was a man much given to joy and laughter.

"Dyflin is our home, Astrid, no matter how stubbornly you fight it. It is our birthright and it is where we belong."

Astrid's blood boiled despite the bite of the winter air in the harbor. Grinding her jaw to keep from shouting at her brother—for that would only make matters worse—she fought for calm with every word.

"I will never feel at home while we crawl like worms before a foreign king. His men will return, and they'll try to foist another heifer on you."

"I'm going to tell Cara you said that," Sitric grinned.

Astrid shoved him gently, as they'd done since childhood when teasing one another. "She'll never believe you," Astrid shot back. "And you can't use her to avoid the problem at hand."

He sighed, gazing once more over the waters. "I want to marry for alliance as much as I want to witness Ragnarok, but I cannot delay much longer."

"Then why do we not act against Brian sooner rather than later?" she demanded. "So he won one battle. Why let him win the war?"

"We need time and resources to rebuild," Sitric replied with enviable calm. "We lost many men. It will be years before we can gather an even greater force and try again. We must bide our time and defend our legacy as best we can while we wait for another opportunity."

"What of mercenaries?" Astrid tried. "We have gold enough from trade."

"I will not empty our coffers for a war that we will lose. Even with mercenaries, we are not prepared to battle with Brian. Not yet."

She opened her mouth to argue further, but Sitric held up a hand.

"I applaud your cleverness and courage, but I tire of repeating this argument over and over with you." He took her hands in his, no doubt to soften the blow. He'd always been too kind for his own good, too worried over the feelings of others to follow his own ambitions. "Dyflin is your home, dear sister. And it's time to make the best of it."

What more could she say? Instead of pressing her brother, Astrid watched the sails hold taut against the strong winds. When she was young, she'd been so afraid they would buckle in the whipping wind, but Sitric always reminded her that they were made to hold the wind. They were strong.

Just like she needed to be.

When they returned to the shore from the rowers' practice, Sitric walked beside Astrid on the journey back to their fortress.

"Perhaps you, too, should consider a marriage," her bold brother suggested, as though that wasn't the stupidest solution she'd ever heard. "Take a husband, have some children. Perhaps then you would feel you had a home."

"If I traveled north, perhaps I might," Astrid replied with great strength of will. "But I have no use for a husband from this land. My children will learn the ways of our ancestors, not a random blending of the two cultures."

Sitric chuckled deep and low.

"What do you find funny about that?" Astrid demanded in outrage.

"You yourself are a random blending of the two cultures, are you not? How quickly you forget your grandsire was one of those squabbling kings you so loathe."

What could she say to such a jab? Sitric was correct, that their mother had been sired by a king of Éire on an Ostman slave woman.

Strained silence descended on the long walk through the center of the bustling market town, at least on Astrid's part. Sitric made conversation with his men, the team that had been rowing the longship across the harbor to keep their *viking* skills sharp.

They passed house after house on the trek up the winding hillside, many built in the style of her people, but just as many built in the native style of Éire. It didn't bother her that the two peoples coexisted in Dyflin. No, Astrid understood the necessity to grasp at something approximating peace in the settlement.

The inequities bothered her. Freydis, her childhood friend, married a Gael and now dressed and spoke as one of them, her babes fluent only in the native tongue. Finn, one of Brian's Fianna warriors who stayed with them during the marriage negotiations, may know the traditions and language of his Ostman father, but his skills and behaviors placed him squarely in the camp of the Gaels.

All the men Sitric had suggested for her betrothals came from Éire, which was well and good for someone who wanted to blend into this new land. From everything she observed, to do so was to sign the death warrant of Ostman heritage, to agree to abandon the very culture she grasped toward so desperately.

She couldn't avoid her brother's betrothals forever, but Astrid would be damned if he thought she would ever marry a Gael.

CHAPTER TWO

"**A**GAIN!" CORMAC SHOUTED, grinning like a fool.

Once more, young Duncan rushed him.

Once more, the lad hesitated when he reached Cormac. All the power of his charge disappeared when he swung his sword.

"You're not afraid to hit me, are you, boy? My sister hits harder than you."

Duncan's face reddened, his beardless jaw clenching in anger. The young prince's swordskill had improved greatly over the past few years, but he still lacked the power needed to keep him alive in battle. And at fifteen summers, he'd fight in the next one.

All the Fianna, the band of elite warriors who served King Brian Boru of Mumhain, helped train the king's son. But this morn was the last opportunity for Cormac to teach the boy before he left with the Fianna for Dyflin, to winter there on a political mission. Knowing that Duncan may well see battle before he saw Cormac next, Cormac pushed him hard.

Duncan charged again. This time, Cormac saw the wildness in his brown eyes. Duncan's practice sword came down. Cormac parried, their weapons clanking loudly. This time, Duncan didn't stop when his stroke fell. Again and again and again, his sword thrust toward Cormac, until he had to stop to catch his breath.

"You were angry, aye?" Cormac asked while Duncan bent over, heaving.

He nodded.

"That is how you should attack a man, but don't be angry

when you do it."

"Why not?" Duncan asked. "I did better, didn't I?"

"Anger makes you fast and foolish. Keep the technique, but abandon the emotion behind it. Hit through your stroke; don't stop when you reach your mark."

Breathing normally again, Duncan stood and swung his sword through several practice strokes. "What will I do while you're gone?"

"Run," Cormac answered easily. "You need better stamina for a battle. And make Abban practice with you every day." He pointed a finger at Duncan to emphasize his orders. "Every. Single. Day. You understand?"

Duncan nodded. "Stab Abban every day and then run away."

"Your first battle is on the horizon, and you must survive it if you want to join the Fianna one day."

"I'm fifteen, Cormac," Duncan groaned. "You can stop worrying. My father was fourteen when he raided Luimneach."

"He was twenty-seven," Cormac countered with a laugh at the bold lie. "And it matters not. I'll never stop worrying over you."

It was the truth, though he spoke it lightly. Duncan wasn't his relative by blood, but Cormac considered him a nephew all the same. Cormac's eldest sister had raised the boy, and Cormac had lived at Caiseal since Duncan's birth. Earlier, even. He'd learned long ago that blood didn't make a family.

The monastery bell rang for morning prayers, and Cormac stood to return to the fortress proper. "Time to go," he told Duncan. "Don't want to be late."

They climbed the hill back to the fortress at Caiseal, the Rock as some called it, to find Diarmid, his youngest brother, and Finn, another warrior in Brian's band of Fianna, jesting in the courtyard. His brother guffawed so loudly at something Finn said that even the horses waiting beside them turned to look. As the two men laughed and spoke, it seemed they hadn't a single concern over their upcoming journey east. Illadan, the leader of the

Fianna, watched them from the feasting hall's steps.

Cormac sighed heavily, glancing toward the greying eastern sky. Dark, angry clouds chased the sun toward the western horizon, no doubt bent on drowning them before the day's end. At least Brian allowed them use of two of his carriages for the women. Narrowing his eyes at the coming storm, Cormac only hoped the carriages were watertight.

They couldn't wait much longer to leave if they wanted to make any progress toward Dyflin today. By the looks of it, the rain would be heavy enough to wash out the road, or at the very least slow them considerably.

"Ready to leave," Cormac ordered his two companions on his way past them and into the feasting hall.

Inside, he found the rest of their traveling party chatting merrily around the central hearth, as though they weren't running late at all. Sláine, the youngest daughter of King Brian Boru of Mumhain, waved to him as he entered. Catrin, younger sister of the Lady Cara, who had recently accepted his brother Diarmid's proposal of marriage amidst quite a scandal—the sort of scandal that only his devilish younger brother could cause, was too invested in some story she told to notice his approach.

King Brian and Queen Dunla, Cormac's elder sister, fare-welled the two women. Dunla's marriage to Brian had been the last attempt to forge a peace between Cormac's father, King Cahill of Connachta, and the ambitious King of Mumhain. Cormac's chest still ached every time he thought of that night when his father had left them.

Tall of stature and grey-haired, Brian was well into the later years of his life, though he managed it well enough to continue riding to battle with his men. Dunla, on the other hand, was only middle-aged, her black hair peppered with grey but her skin still smooth with youth. Cormac had questioned his sister's marriage to a man so much her senior, even a man so kind as Brian, but Dunla radiated joy and contentment. It had been clear from very early in their marriage that Dunla was happy with her choice of husband, odd though it may seem to some.

"Cormac," Brian called when he noticed his foster son's appearance in the hall, "walk with me a moment."

Cormac did as his king bid, accompanying him on a circuitous route through the back of the hall that eventually would bring them to the courtyard.

"I have a matter that must be handled with tact and delicacy," Brian began. "I am sending two women in appearance only, to appease Sitric with the illusion of a choice in the matter of his bride."

Cormac looked askance at the aged king. A thousand questions formed in his mind, but he knew better than to interrupt. Instead he held his tongue and nodded his understanding.

"Sitric must marry Sláine. If he is wise, he will see the political advantage for him in choosing her over Catrin, but Sitric has ever an unpredictable temperament. I feel the choice should be obvious, but I need you and Illadan to ensure he, too, sees it that way."

The task suited Diarmed best, though Cormac fully understood why the king hadn't asked for him. His brother's love affair with the first bride Brian sent to Sitric had gotten them into this mess in the first place. Their family name would lose all value to Brian if they failed him in this a second time.

"You have my word," Cormac assured him. "I will see it done."

Brian inclined his head in a gesture of acknowledgement. "Don't hesitate to remind Sitric that a betrothal was one of the terms of our peace. Should he forfeit the marriage, he will also forfeit the peace. My patience with him is nearing its end."

Cormac hoped it wouldn't come to that. He'd grown fond of the affable Ostman over the course of their many meetings. If Brian sent men to subdue him again, Cormac and the Fianna would be among them. The thought soured his mood considerably, fueling his resolve to get Sitric married with all haste.

They left Caiseal before the ill wind brought the clouds to

meet them. Unfortunately, Dyflin lay east of Caiseal—which meant they rode straight into the storm.

The four Fianna warriors rode on horseback. Cormac and Illadan took the lead, Finn rode beside the carriages, and Diarmid watched the back. Sláine and Catrin shared one of the small carriages. Their lady's maids rode in the other. The carriage drivers managed the reins in determined silence, no doubt as anxious as Cormac to be through this weather.

Though Cormac didn't relish the thought of returning to Dyflin and the acerbic Astrid, he preferred it to traveling in a winter storm. Snow fell rarely, but the rain that poured from the heavens at every opportunity held enough chill to compensate. The journey should take but two days at a leisurely pace, even with the carriages. On their own, the Fianna could make the journey in a single day. But as the first drops of rain portended the coming onslaught, Cormac worried the journey would be as long as it was miserable.

With naught else to occupy his thoughts, they turned toward the arrival at Dyflin. Sitric's meddlesome sister would no doubt tear into him the moment they arrived. Cormac had never met a more discontented person, man or woman. She seemed intent on harassing him at every opportunity, though she got on just fine with his brothers and Finn. What quality he held that she so disdained he couldn't begin to guess. All he knew was that to the best of his ability, he needed to avoid Astrid. She had a way of making him lose his patience—the thing in which he took the greatest pride.

The first day's journey, an affair that lasted all of six hours, went better than expected. Aye, it was slow going between the rain and wind and meager daylight hours this time of the year. But compared with that night it was downright pleasant.

The wind picked up first, just as they settled into camp for the night. It whipped the horses' manes and shook the leaves above them in a fit of wintry rage. Cormac, Diarmid, Illadan, and Finn slept side by side for warmth, wrapped in their cloaks and blankets. The women bedded down in their carriages, doing their best to keep the cold at bay.

HOURS LATER, CORMAC woke to shouting. He shot up from his blankets, wiping the sleep from his eyes and searching for the source of the commotion.

It didn't take long to find it.

Though darkness yet devoured the land, moonlight illuminated the two carriages. Only one of them stood upright.

Diarmid and Illadan already tore through the debris of the front carriage, which lay on its side. How the first had toppled in the gales wasn't as much a mystery as how the second still stood.

Beside Cormac, Finn jumped to his feet and together they hurried to help.

"Sláine!" Cormac called, his heart pounding. "Sláine are you in there?"

Sláine was as a sister to him, having grown up in the same household. Indeed, he knew her better than he did his own sister.

"Sláine!" Diarmid echoed, his voice frantic.

The door to the second carriage opened.

"It's alright." Sláine stepped out, followed by Catrin and their maids. "We were so cold we went to their carriage in the night."

Cormac exhaled sharply, relief washing over him like the ceaseless rain. Thank the Lord the women were safe. The drivers had slept near the horses to keep them calm through the stormy night, so no one had been injured.

"Can we fix it?" Cormac asked Ailill, one of the men.

Ailill grimaced, shaking his head. "Not without tools and new wood."

"Can the horse handle the extra passengers?" Cormac would hate for the maids to ride in the frigid rain.

"Normally, aye," Ailill answered. "But with the roads the way they are, it may be too much weight."

"Let's try it. Ladies, make yourselves comfortable in there. It's going to be tight." He turned next to Ailill. "Get the horses ready. It's time to keep moving." Finally, he looked toward Diarmid and Finn. "Let's see about retrieving their trunks and moving this off the road."

He thought that convincing Sitric to marry Sláine would be the hardest part of the mission. As of now, it appeared getting her there in the first place may prove the greater challenge.

CHAPTER THREE

"**T**HEY'RE HERE!" THE shout rang up from the guards posted at the gates of their holding, drawing Astrid reluctantly out into the rain.

It had been raining for four days now. Day or night, it made no difference, and the deluge showed no signs of stopping.

Pulling her ermine-lined cloak over her head, she stepped out of her brother's hall far enough to be within shouting range of the guards. "How long?" she yelled.

"Under an hour!" he called back.

Retreating to the warm hall—one of two in their holding—Astrid ordered hot baths drawn for their guests. She may not want anything to do with Brian or his Fianna or his parade of brides, but as one of the ladies of this house it fell to her to host them properly.

Unfortunately.

Astrid had just returned from relaying the news of their companions' return to the Fianna who had remained in Dyflin when the travelers arrived. Looking quite a bit worse for wear.

The door to the main hall burst open, the sound of rain and wind drowning out all else. Cormac stepped through first, covered in dirt and soaked to the bone, and Astrid's blood pounded in her veins. That man drove her insane.

When first he'd come to Dyflin weeks ago, his striking figure and handsome face took her breath away. Then she'd had the displeasure of spending time with him. He was too quiet. Too calculating. Utterly unnerving. The man did naught but watch everyone else, deciding his next move in eerie silence. And Astrid knew, beyond a doubt, that *he* was the one who had the best chance at making a fool of her brother.

Behind him were four women, two dressed like nobles of Éire and two in plainer clothes. The taller of the two nobles had hair the color of a good ale—a deep, rich golden brown. A jewel-encrusted circlet sat upon her brow, the emerald gems matching her sodden dress.

The other noble looked more child than woman. Astrid doubted she had sixteen summers if she had one. She wore a wine-red dress—a hue that Astrid could never wear with her own aggressively red hair. The woman's ebony locks and sharp features seemed familiar to Astrid, but she couldn't decide why. She'd certainly never seen any of the women before.

Past the women, three more Fianna—Diarmid, Illadan, and Finn—stepped inside and pulled the door hastily closed.

Sitric stood from where he'd been waiting near the hearth, striding with a wide grin to greet them all. "Welcome, welcome!" His booming voice carried across the crowded hall. "I take it your quest went well?" He tilted his head questioningly toward Diarmid.

That particular Fianna, her brother's favorite for their similar dispositions, had stolen Cara, the first bride sent by Brian, from her brother. As Sitric wasn't keen on marrying in the first place, and his good friend deeply loved the woman, they had managed to move past it.

But her brother's betrothal wasn't simply a gesture; it was a requirement. And Diarmid had ruined Brian's proposed match, forcing him to make the journey back to Caiseal and deliver the news to his king in person.

"Well enough," Diarmid grinned, pulling Sitric into an enthusiastic embrace.

Astrid shook her head at their antics, but couldn't keep the ghost of a smile from her lips. At least they lived their lives in joy.

"We have more news," Cormac added, scanning the room. When his gaze found hers, he turned back to Sitric as though he'd been burned.

Normally, such a reaction would insult Astrid. In Cormac, however, it gave her a smug satisfaction at the notion that perhaps she intimidated him. That man needed to be put in his place anyway.

Sitric waved away Cormac's statement. "We have time enough to speak of business. Get cleaned up, get settled, and then we shall speak further."

Cormac's jaw tightened, but he didn't argue with her brother. Instead he nodded, stepped to the side, and gestured at the woman in the green gown with hair the color of the ash tree's heartwood.

"We bring with us Sláine ingen Briain, Princess of Mumhain," his hand moved to the raven-haired girl, "and Catrin, Princess of Thurles."

Astrid smiled inwardly. That was why the girl looked familiar—she was the younger sister of Cara, of whom she'd grown fond in these past weeks.

Her brother smiled outwardly, his grin somehow growing to engulf his entire face. "You are my dearest Cara's sister, are you not?" He stepped toward Catrin, hugging her and then Sláine in turn. "You are both most welcome in Dyflin."

Poor Catrin nodded, clearly unsure how to proceed. She was rescued by the appearance of Cara from the back of the hall, who hurried to greet her sister. Unlike Sitric, Cara did not pull her sodden sibling into an exuberant hug. Instead, she helped fix the stray locks of dark hair that had fallen out of place, fussing like a mother hen over the girl's general state of disarray.

The journey must have been arduous indeed, for two princesses to appear thusly for presentation to a king. Though Cormac hadn't yet said as much, Astrid was no fool. She knew these women were Brian's next attempt to see her brother wed.

As Astrid watched her brother play nice with their new

guests, exchanging smiles and laughs, tossing compliments about like ships on the sea, the room closed in around her. She felt the world tilt and spin, as though she alone were trapped in this horrific fantasy and no matter how loud she yelled, no one tried to stop it.

Her brother could not marry either of these women. Catrin was but a child, and heir to land that Sitric already owned. It would serve no purpose whatsoever. Sláine would bind her brother irrevocably to Brian. Wedding Brian's own daughter was as good as climbing into his lap like a hound and begging for scraps. Nay, neither woman would do.

The problem identified, Astrid now required a solution. She could speak with her brother, but she'd tried that a few days ago on the longship and he'd been wholly unreceptive to her concerns.

Or, she could speak with Cormac and try to cut the head off the snake. Maybe she could scare him off before the negotiations began. It felt an insurmountable task, but she had to try something. And Astrid never backed down from a challenge.

If her brother wanted her to make the best of being trapped in a foreign kingdom, Astrid would begin by dealing with this wife problem.

She intercepted Cormac on his way down the hall toward his room, starting right in before he could run off. "What are you doing here with those women?"

"Why must you plague me, woman? I have seven other companions you could torment instead." The look of resignation on his strong features was almost endearing.

"You're the one in charge."

"Illadan is the one in charge," he corrected. "I am his second."

"Illadan is the one in charge of the men." She pointed a finger at him. "You're the one in charge of the decisions. The quietest men are the ones doing the plotting."

He ran a hand down his face, exhaling loudly. "So you're harassing me because I keep to myself? That hardly seems a fair assessment."

"I'm harassing you because I know you're trouble."

"You and I have different ideas of trouble." He made to step around her.

Astrid intercepted him again. "He's not going to marry either of them."

"That choice lays with Sitric."

"You're wasting your time," she insisted, hoping the vehemence in her tone would convince him of the truth of her words.

"Are you not in charge of the household, sister?" Her brother appeared beside them, though she hadn't noticed his approach. "These men look weary. We should let them rest before we battle them, else the fight will not be fair and the victory hollow at best."

"Of course," she acquiesced tightly. Plastering on a smile dripping with irritation, she turned to Cormac. "Allow me to take you to the baths."

It took every ounce of her will to do as her brother bid her, leading the guests to their waiting baths and showing the ladies to their rooms.

When she stepped away from delivering Cormac, he blocked her path as she had his. Piercing azure eyes burned right through her, sending a shiver down her spine.

"I know what you're trying to do," he growled, "but I'm not going to give up because of some meddlesome woman." He leaned down toward her, so that she felt the warmth of his face before her. "I'm going to win."

CHAPTER FOUR

THAT WOMAN WAS trying to kill him. No, not woman. That felt far too generous a term for the infuriating, conniving, irrational creature who insisted on following him about and thwarting his every move. Loudly. Like one of those shrieking creatures from the stories that Cara so loved. What were they called?

Ah, yes.

That harpy was trying to kill him.

The warm bath waters felt incredible. The luxury of a hot bath, unshared with his companions, did not go beyond Cormac's notice. The harpy might be intent on shutting down the marriage negotiations, but it impressed him that her bitterness didn't impact her hospitality. If you could call constant confrontation hospitality, that was.

Cormac had already stayed in Dyflin for over a fortnight before they'd traveled to Caiseal and back, so he'd grown accustomed to Astrid's antics. For whatever reason, he served as her main target, though he and Illadan shared leadership of the Fianna with Broccan. It was a pity her temperament matched her fiery locks, for Cormac always held a weakness for red-haired beauties.

He needed to speak with Sitric privately, before his sister could poison his thoughts further. The King of Dyflin was a reasonable man, though capricious. If Cormac could explain the situation calmly and privately, 'twould be easily resolved.

Though the steaming water tempted him to linger, Cormac hurried to wash and dress so that he could hunt down Sitric before Astrid did. All of his men enjoyed their time in the Ostman settlement, the games plenty and their cares few. But Cormac could never truly relax, knowing that he need but step around the next corner and the red-haired devil would accost him. She didn't intimidate him as much as she unnerved him. More than anything, Cormac hated losing control of his sensibilities—a thing that happened nearly every time he encountered her.

After his bath, Cormac found Sitric in the family hall, speaking with his mother and sister. The king's holding in Dyflin consisted of a scattering of buildings ringed by a tall wooden fence and gate. Two halls, one for the family and one for guests, stood proudly in the center of the enclosure. Stables, kitchens, servants' quarters, and the like lay beyond the halls.

The two halls were identical in design, each consisting of a long rectangular room flanked by individual rooms on the two longest sides. Doors took up the two shorter walls, and a hearth crackled night and day in the center of the hall. Pillow-covered chairs and benches formed seating areas, neatly tucked into each corner and littered with furs and blankets. Trestle tables and benches filled the rest of the space.

In one of the cozy corners of the family hall, Cormac interrupted a lively conversation between Sitric's family. "Apologies for the intrusion," he began, looking to Sitric, "but I'd like to speak with you at your earliest convenience."

With a sharp look in Astrid's direction, Sitric rose, his smile smaller than it had been when they'd first arrived. "Of course. Let us find a quiet space."

Out the back of the hall, they hurried through the pouring rain and into a small building that served as Sitric's study. Though modest in size, the lush fabrics draped over chairs and the crackling braziers gave it the same comforting quality as the halls. Cormac waited for Sitric to sit, then took his place in the seat opposite. Reclining in leisure, Sitric assessed him from afar before breaking the silence.

"I know what you would say."

"Aye, you do," Cormac agreed. "But I know not your thoughts."

With measured words, Sitric turned to him. "I understand that Brian wants me wed to a bride from his kingdom. But I don't want either of the ones he's sent."

Cormac nodded, playing the part of the sympathetic friend. And, for Cormac's part, it wasn't entirely an act. "He's concerned that you intend to break the truce."

"I have no such intentions," Sitric asserted. "But sending me the choice of a pup or his own daughter—tell me you see the manipulation, Cormac."

"Many a king has asked for Sláine's hand. A man could do worse than become a son of Brian Boru. Perhaps he intended it as a sign of respect, an invitation to become family."

"Or he trusts me so little that he must leash me like one of his hounds," Sitric shot him an apologetic grimace. "No offense, of course."

"None taken. The Hound of the Ulaid was one of the fiercest warriors in all Éire. To be likened to him is an honor."

Sitric's chuckle gave Cormac hope, but his words quickly dashed it. "My oath is not enough for him, so he must shackle me into obedience. For how could I make war on my wife's kin?"

"Easily, as it turns out." Cormac couldn't keep the bitterness from his voice. "Brian wed my sister when I was no older than Catrin, yet both continue to invade one another. Believe me, Brian knows better than any man how little the bonds of kinship can dissuade violence, for either party."

"Then why give the illusion of choice?" Sitric groaned. "If it was meant as a gesture of friendship, why not send only Sláine?"

Damn. Sitric had him there. "I speak only what I see," Cormac told him. "His intentions are as unknown to me as they are you."

"Astrid remains bitter over our defeat last winter," Sitric

began, surprising Cormac, "yet it is hard to deny the truth of her words."

Of course. Cormac sat perfectly still, giving no outward sign of his feelings on the topic. Inside, he wanted to hit the training yard with Conan. *Of course* she'd wasted no time in turning her brother against them. Brian should find a way to recruit her to their cause and sic her upon his other foes. Cormac had no doubt she'd wear them down.

"And what are her words?" Cormac asked evenly. He'd mastered any outbursts of temper long ago. Except, apparently, where Astrid was concerned.

Sitric looked upward, then spoke as though recounting her phrasing exactly. "It's bad enough that we've spent this long entertaining Brian's hounds. The last thing you should do is join them." He laughed. "She also told me that should I marry either woman, I will be little more than a puppet to a king gone mad with ambition. Oh, and—my personal favorite—submitting to his demands will rob me of what honor I have left after that horrendous routing."

"That sounds about right." Cormac smiled, deliberately making light of her words. "And you believe her?"

"I believe she's correct, that it isn't really a choice and that nothing about it bodes well for me or my kingdom. But, it was her solution that caught my attention."

Cormac sat up straighter. "She proposed a solution?"

"Aye. She thought I might find a suitable bride of *my* choosing, to marry with Brian's approval."

It wasn't terrible, Cormac had to admit, but it wasn't the mission. He'd sworn to Brian to see Sitric wed Sláine, and he wasn't leaving Dyflin until he fulfilled his oath.

"Your silence concerns me," Sitric remarked. "You don't think it's a good plan? Either that, or you are withholding information from me."

Cormac sighed. He hated threatening people, especially people he'd come to consider friends. "He made it clear that should neither woman be chosen, the treaty would be void."

Sitric's grin fell from his face. "I remain undecided."

And Cormac remained unsurprised. "Take your time," he offered. "It's an important decision, and I've no desire to travel again until the weather improves."

Brian hadn't given the mission a time limit, so Cormac held no concern on that front. Nay, his concerns about staying rested solely on how long he could survive the harassment of a certain redheaded princess.

CHAPTER FIVE

A STRID FASTENED THE brooches onto her sapphire blue apron dress, one of her favorites. Even though it didn't match her eyes, it complimented her scarlet hair. Most folk had blue or brown or green eyes. A few had gray. Astrid was the only person she knew with eyes the color of honey. Occasionally her brother told her they tinged with palest green, like the peridot gems that passed through the shipyard, but most folk told her they looked like the amber liquid that gave them mead for the long winter nights.

Smoothing her gown and checking her plaits, she opened her door to join the boisterous crowd gathering to dine. Sitric abhorred simplicity. Aye, though they didn't slaughter a boar for every meal, every dinner was an event regardless of the fare being served. Upon entering the bustling hall, Astrid found it just as chaotic as she expected.

She took her seat near the end of the table beside Niamh, a skilled healer who traveled with her husband, the Fianna warrior Dallan, and served as lady's maid to Princess Cara. With the arrival of two new princesses, even the massive trestle table now felt crowded.

Sitric sat at the head of the table near her. Their mother held forth at the other. Across from Astrid, the eight Fianna sat shoulder-to-shoulder in a row. She smiled to herself when she noted that Cormac had chosen the seat on the very end, furthest from her. Perhaps her intimidation tactics held merit.

It mattered not, however, because Sitric appeared swayed by her arguments this afternoon in favor of proposing a different bride to Brian. She'd come up with it during the course of their conversation, and it had intrigued him. He even seemed to agree with her assessment of the two women Brian sent. Overall, the conversation couldn't have gone better.

Now all she had to do was continue monitoring the situation, prepared to step back in should her brother's feelings change.

The meal was modest, not a proper feast by any means but neither was it scant. Cod chewets and a bean and vegetable stew were the bulk of the dinner, with warm, fresh bread and a few bowls of skyr. A low hum of chatter threaded through the room as everyone caught up on the goings-on of the past few days. Everything went smoothly, until Princess Catrin joined the conversation shortly after the ale pitchers were refreshed.

"I hear you are looking to marry, my lord," the young woman said boldly to Sitric. "I wondered what qualities you value in a woman?"

Down the table, Cara coughed delicately.

Astrid couldn't have been more pleased. At this rate, she'd hardly have to interfere at all.

Sitric took the improper question in stride, ever ready for a new game. "I'm considering marriage, yes, but I wouldn't say I'm looking for it. And as for your second query, I should like a bride who is honest and adventurous."

"And let us not forget courageous, strong of will, and honorable," Astrid added.

"Yes, of course," Sitric agreed hastily. "Those as well."

"I was surprised to hear you had never been married," Catrin continued, undeterred. Beside her, Cara's face flushed, her lips thinning into a tight line.

Astrid choked down a laugh, not wanting to cause any more of a scene. The ignorant princess implied that Sitric was either old or unsuitable for marriage, though Astrid doubted Catrin realized those implications.

Her brother would never wed so naive a woman, and convincing him of the problems with Sláine should prove simple.

"My brother only has thirty summers," Astrid informed her gently. "Some men wait longer even than that to wed."

Finally, Catrin's face blushed to match her mortified sister's. "Oh!" she exclaimed breathily. "I didn't mean to imply—"

"Astrid, are you not of an age for your own marriage?"

Astrid's gaze shot like an arrow toward the end of the table. Cormac's eyes twinkled with the mischief of his calculated interruption. The lopsided smirk on his face didn't do her temper any favors, either.

"Don't tell me you're interested?" she whipped back.

Cormac choked on his ale. "Not in the least. I simply wondered why Sitric here is the constant target of marriage alliances, while you appear happily unwed."

"An interesting point, my friend," Sitric agreed, his fingers stroking his golden beard thoughtfully. "In fact, my sister and I spoke of this very topic earlier."

Cormac's crooked smile grew to a victorious grin. "Did you now?"

She had a thing or two to say to him once the table cleared out.

"Aye, I feel it's time for Astrid to wed."

"No suitable men have presented themselves," Astrid explained. "Like my brother, I, too, have requirements for an adequate partner."

"Perhaps, like your brother, we can help find you a suitable match." Cormac's eyes never left hers, spearing her in place. Challenging her.

Her heart pounded, its volume rising alongside her ire. "I doubt it."

"Brian has many sons," Cormac goaded. "I'd be happy to brave the deluge to retrieve one of them for you."

Astrid's temples throbbed, her fingers reaching to massage them. "When I deign to wed, it will be to an Ostman. And certainly no relative of your king's."

"He's your king, too, is he not?" Cormac pressed.

Her brother inserted himself, no doubt to cease the questioning of their loyalty to Brian. "Unfortunately, dear sister, our friend here has a point. It is time for you to marry, and you will marry a Gael to further tie us to this land and its people."

"But—" Astrid started right in with her protest, but Sitric wouldn't allow it.

"We've discussed this numerous times," his voice softened, "and I am decided. But," he announced to the room, "I am not without a heart. My sister desires to wed one of our people to preserve her ties to our culture. Luckily for us, *Jól* is near."

Astrid couldn't fathom what the feast of midwinter had to do with her marriage. Before she could ask, Sitric continued.

"*Jól* is a time of festivity, games, and community. A perfect opportunity to share our culture with your future husband."

Astrid tired of this nonsense. "What is your point, brother?"

"We will send messengers across Éire, inviting select men to come to Dyflin for *Jól*. For a full turning of the moon, we will host a *leikmót*."

Every Fianna warrior turned to Finn, who took pity on them and translated under his breath. "A festival of games."

"Only the foreigners will compete, but they must learn the Ostman games to do so. The winner—who proves himself the most Ostman of the Gaels—will win your hand."

Astrid's stomach dropped, her ears buzzing as the blood rushed to her head. "You cannot be serious!"

"It's the perfect compromise," Sitric declared. "You marry a Gael who will not rob you of your heritage. Everyone wins. And we all get to enjoy a month of games."

Catrin and Sláine hurried to add their enthusiastic support to Sitric's absurd plan. Astrid's efforts to protest were drowned in a sea of excitement at the prospect of the games. Her brother stood, raising his hand for silence. The room obeyed.

"It is decided. The *leikmót* begins in a fortnight. The prize is my sister."

CHAPTER SIX

S HE SHOOK WITH anger, her face nearly as red as her hair. Had it been anyone else, Cormac would've regretted the turn in conversation. He hadn't meant to pin a betrothal on her, simply to turn conversation away from Sitric's choice of bride.

Catrin had fumbled through a disaster of a conversation, embarrassing not only herself but the Fianna as well. He'd watched Cara do her best discreet intervention to no avail before deciding a change of topic was in order. Little had he known that Astrid's unwed state was a topic of dissent in the family.

Sitric's proposal seemed eminently reasonable. As he'd said, it would be the best of both their desires in a husband for Astrid: a man who respects her culture and a man to help their political position in Éire. It didn't surprise Cormac in the least that Sitric's solution managed to include games.

The best part of the whole ordeal was that Astrid would now be occupied with delaying her own betrothal. Hopefully that meant she'd stay out of Sitric's.

He'd already spoken with Sitric directly about marrying Sláine, but Cormac remained unconvinced that Sitric intended to cooperate. With Astrid finally out of his way, Cormac could focus his efforts on others who held Sitric's respect. Two people came to mind instantly: Diarmid, Sitric's good friend, and Gormla, Sitric's mother.

After the dinner itself ended, folks went their separate ways. The Fianna and Sitric's warriors stayed at the table to game and drink. Townsfolk who'd attended the meal returned to their homes. Some of the women of the household stayed to play, but more of them left to retire for the night.

Cormac sat at the table while ale was refilled and knuckle-bones brought out, listening to the general merriment of his companions. Then he spotted Gormla. She left their table and Cormac excused himself, hurrying to catch her before she disappeared into her room.

"My lady," he called, halting her near the end of the hall.

Gormla turned, her expression warming when she spotted her pursuer. "Cormac. What can I do for you?"

Gormla and Astrid could've been twins but for age and eye color. Where Astrid's tresses glowed like smoldering embers, Gormla's resembled a rich wine. And where Astrid's eyes were orbs of amber, Gormla's were the same pale blue as Sitric's.

"I hoped to speak with you for a moment." Cormac gestured to the nearest seating area, blessedly unoccupied, and they each took a chair. He waited until she got comfortable before easing into the conversation. "I wanted to extend my gratitude for allowing my men and I to impose upon you and your family for so long a stay."

Gormla snorted in amusement. "No, you wish to know my thoughts on the marriage of my son."

"Aye, but my thanks are genuine." Cormac appreciated di-rectness, but he didn't want to appear dismissive of his generous host.

"You should know that what I think hardly matters. My chil-dren know better than to take marriage advice from me."

Now it was Cormac's turn to scoff. "Surely the experience can only be a boon."

When Gormla's first husband, Sitric and Astrid's father, died, she began a torrid affair with Brian that ended in a son and a failed marriage. Their relationship crashed through Caiseal like a storm, all lightning and thunder between the occasional calm. After it inevitably ended, Gormla returned to Dyflin to live with her older children while her younger son, Duncan, underwent his fosterage. It all happened during Cormac's fosterage, so he'd spoken with Gormla on numerous occasions but rarely on any topic of great import.

"Even if they agreed with you on that, they both feel I've too great a personal history with Brian to judge the situation fairly. And they're likely right to think so."

Cormac nodded, considering his next move. "You know Brian," he agreed. "And you know how he can be when he sets his mind to something. Or when he takes offense with someone."

All mirth fled her face. "It's gone that far, then, has it?"

"I am here to fulfill my oath to him, aye. But I am also here to prevent further bloodshed between my friend and my foster father." He leaned forward, elbows resting on his thighs. "I fear Sitric doesn't see the threat behind the request, and that your daughter's voice is louder than any other in his ear."

Gormla considered him, leaning back against the dark furs and crossing her arms. "Brian always spoke of your wisdom," she began thoughtfully, surprising Cormac. "Not only your ability to observe without prejudice but to then use your observations to better understand people. Tell me, why do you think my daughter speaks so loudly?"

Cormac searched his mind, running through his observations of Astrid.

Loud. Angry. Stubborn. Proud.

He realized quickly that for all his observing, not once had he done so without prejudice. Perhaps his efforts with her failed not only because of her temperament, but also because he'd never genuinely tried to win her over.

"I'll help you," she offered when he didn't answer. "My Astrid can be a challenge to understand, but more often than not, she's motivated by fear."

"I highly doubt that," Cormac countered. 'Fearless' might be one of the most complimentary words he'd use to describe her.

"Then you have more observing to do. If you want her on

your side, that is."

"While I have your ear, what advice do you have regarding your son?" Cormac had more ideas where Sitric was concerned, but it could never hurt to hear a mother's insights. Already he felt this conversation could be the turning point in his mission.

Then Astrid appeared.

For the first time in the history of their acquaintance, she didn't glare at him when she stopped beside his chair.

"Astrid, dear," Gormla cooed, "I thought you'd gone to bed."

"I had." She swallowed hard, then turned to Cormac. "But then I thought of a conversation we had earlier, and I wish to continue our discussion."

If Cormac hadn't been sitting, he would have fallen over. Was Astrid truly seeking him out for a reasonable discussion of the brides? He stood, not about to miss such an opportunity.

"Don't bother moving," Gormla insisted, standing from her own seat. "I was about to turn in anyway."

She gave Astrid a quick hug on her way to her room. Astrid took her mother's abandoned chair, facing Cormac and scanning the room behind him.

He waited, letting her lead the conversation since she'd been the one to request it.

As soon as Gormla was out of sight, Astrid's face flushed crimson, her hands clenching into tight fists. "This is all *your* fault," she ground out. "You pushed my brother into this, now *you* need to get me out of it."

He didn't know what he'd expected, but he certainly wasn't surprised. "Discussing the possible marriage of a princess, especially when her brother is to be wed, is not unreasonable. I need to do nothing."

"I thought you Fianna were supposed to be men of honor." Her voice rose higher with every word. "How is it honorable to help entrap a woman in a marriage against her will?"

Cormac hated the feeling of guilt that slammed into him at her accusation, but he wasn't about to get entangled in a family matter—especially *this* family. "Did Sitric not say you'd already spoken of it before? Numerous times, if memory serves. Nay, princess, I think that dam was broken long before I joined the conversation."

To his astonishment and amusement, her face reddened deeper, now nearly matching the color of her tresses. Her rounded nose flared dangerously. Cormac braced for the next onslaught.

Instead, Astrid surprised him.

"What of a truce?" she grumbled, not sounding the least enthusiastic at the prospect. "If you won't be decent, perhaps I can compensate you in some way."

Cormac sat back in his chair. "Consider me intrigued."

"Well, I'm not going to do all your work for you. Tell me what it is you want."

"I'm the one here with nothing to lose," he countered, enjoying finally having the upper hand in one of their arguments. "Let's hear *your* proposal."

Astrid huffed and brought a hand to her temple, massaging the idea into existence. If she weren't such a thoroughly disagreeable and damnably frustrating woman, she'd be exactly the sort that caught Cormac's attention. Red hair. Delicate features. A fierce personality. Aye, it was a good thing that she hated him and he couldn't stand her, otherwise he'd be very tempted by the beautiful Princess of Dyflin.

Quicker than he expected, she looked up at him, her honey-hued eyes sharp as a freshly-honed blade.

"You are," she grimaced, "exactly the sort of man my brother is trying to foist on me. A Gael, a prince with valuable political connections." She waved her hand as though that completed the list of his marriageable qualities. "And I am told you and your men are the best warriors in all the kingdoms."

Cormac did not like where this was going. "I will stop you right there, princess. I cannot marry you, or I would break my oath to Brian."

Her brows, several shades of crimson darker than her hair, furrowed. "But others of your men have wed."

"For love," Cormac explained. "One of our oaths is that we marry for love."

"It matters not," she continued. "We won't be marrying. I want you to compete in the *leikmót* for my hand and win, but then refuse the marriage once the other competitors return home."

"Will your brother not simply summon them back and betroth you to the next man?"

"I have over a month to figure that out, and if we delay long enough with the wedding, perhaps I can convince him otherwise. But for now, this will offer me some small security in my future."

"And what are you offering in exchange for my help?"

She threw him a withering glare. "I will tell my brother whatever you want with regard to the brides sent by Brian. I assume you aim to have him wed Sláine, in which case I will become her greatest champion."

"Deal."

"Excellent." She straightened in her chair.

Cormac knew the conversation wasn't finished when she started worrying her bottom lip. He didn't prompt her, though, as his brothers no doubt would. Instead, he waited.

"You *can* win the *leikmót*, aye?"

Cormac nearly chuckled at the ridiculous question, but then he noted that the color had drained from her face. Her voice had quieted, and she still bit her bottom lip. Gormla was right.

Astrid was afraid.

"Aye," he assured her. "I can win."

CHAPTER SEVEN

THIS WAS ALL his fault. She tugged hard on her cream underdress, the neckline doing its best to make a mess of her braids. Shoving her arms through the sleeves, Astrid reminded herself that she couldn't best Cormac in a duel, and therefore couldn't unleash her anger in that specific way. She doubted any of her men, or even her brother, could beat him, unfortunately. Sighing in resignation, she pulled on her sage green apron dress and fastened the bronze brooches.

She may not be able to punish him properly for his actions, but Astrid wouldn't soon forgive the warrior. She had played nice last night to secure his cooperation, but she blamed him entirely for this disastrous turn of events. Even with their bargain, Astrid's situation remained precarious.

Aye, she had a plan but, as Cormac had pointed out to her, 'twas a faulty one. On top of the threat of an unwanted marriage, Astrid had dug the hole deeper with regard to her brother's arranged marriage. And, as though that weren't enough, she had to manage the planning of these ridiculous games whilst ensuring that Cormac won.

The potent combination of her worries and responsibilities destroyed any appetite she might've had. Instead of breaking her fast in the family's hall, she hurried over to the guest hall in search of Cormac. She had but a fortnight to turn him into a model Ostman.

When she stepped into the hall from the icy mist, Astrid

found it empty, save for Niamh sorting herbs on one of the trestle tables.

"Where is everyone?" she asked, approaching the table and inspecting the array of freshly picked plants. "And whatever are you doing?"

The golden-haired beauty paused in her work. "The men run through the bog every morn, then they train in the yard, then they bathe, then they study. Cormac and Illadan keep them busy, even when they're at their leisure."

"Study?" Astrid repeated. The rest she understood, but that hardly sounded like something expected of a warrior.

"The Fianna must be able to play and perform music and poetry," Niamh explained. "Finn is teaching them the histories of the people, and as a whole they discuss politics and strategy."

"I see," Astrid mumbled, still not understanding in the least why that was a concern of warriors. "And these?" She gestured at the plants covering the table between them.

"Dallan told me the games are quite violent, so I'm making extra salves and tinctures. No one's dying on my watch if I can help it."

"We have healers, you know," Astrid smiled, picking up a sprig of greenery and smelling it. Her nose wrinkled at the acrid scent.

"I know." Niamh caught her gaze. "But I'm better than them."

Astrid chuckled. "I always liked you."

As much as she wanted to linger and watch Niamh's process, she had plenty of her own work waiting. Cormac wouldn't be available until that evening, so she sought out her mother and brother to get started on this ridiculous *leikmót*.

They met in the family's hall, not caring to venture out into the downpour that descended shortly after Astrid left Niamh. Settling into one of the cozy corners, they were left to meet in peace, with naught but the servants passing by on errands.

"I've already dispatched messengers to deliver the invitations to the guests," Sitric began. "Our focus for the next fortnight must be constructing the *leikskálar*. I doubt tents will be sufficient protection from the chill this time of the year, so we'll need to start building the halls as soon as possible to have them ready."

Leikskálar, gaming sheds that housed participants much like miniature halls, were the standard for hosting extended games. It took a great deal of both wood and manpower to see them built, and it sounded as though they were building several.

Astrid narrowed her eyes at her brother. "This is going to cost a fortune. Is it really worth spending all this just to try to get rid of me?"

The smile that held permanent residence on Sitric's bearded face faltered. "You're cleverer than that, sister," he said gently. "Don't let your temper hinder your judgment. You were the one who wanted to move against Brian sooner rather than later, were you not?"

A sinking feeling settled in the pit of her stomach. How had she missed it? "You mean to buy an army through marriage."

"As Brian appears intent on preventing my own marriage from accomplishing such a feat, it falls to you." His smile reappeared, bright as ever. "And the beauty of the games is that it won't seem to Brian that I am deliberately choosing a man who would ally against him."

"And what if a man not of your choosing should win?" Astrid's plans had not changed, not yet at least. But this certainly made a muck into a proper mess.

She *did* want her brother to escape servitude to Brian and become a king unto himself alone. Marrying a man who could give them an army would add speed to the long process, but it wouldn't solve all their problems. And, most importantly, Astrid would still be leaving behind her culture to move to a fully Gaelic kingdom. Alone.

"The only men competing will be those I've invited, and all have advantages to our cause, even those who nominally ally with Brian."

The blood raced through her veins, her mind reaching a conclusion she doubted Cormac would like any more than she did. If Sitric handpicked the men, Cormac would have to convince Sitric to let him join the *leikmót*.

Keeping her features carefully guarded, Astrid pretended irritation to hide her growing concerns.

They spent the next few hours compiling lists of the rules and games, discussing the logistics of feeding so many guests for so long, and debating whether or not they could even get the housing built in time. Astrid doubted it. Gormla thought they might manage it. Sitric saw no problem whatsoever.

Come dinner, Astrid had more to tell Cormac than she thought could fit into one evening of conversation—especially since she'd have to wait until after dinner to corner him. And, somehow, she had to work with him and not attack him at every opportunity. Instead of trying to pull him aside publicly, she decided to retire for the evening and wait for him in his room.

Tonight, she planned to teach him to play *hnefatafl*, a game of cunning much like chess, and an excellent opportunity to thrash him, as Astrid won nearly every game of it she played. She moved the small bedside table to the foot of the bed, setting the board and pieces for a match atop it and looking forward to exacting some revenge upon the warrior, small though it may be.

The interlude felt interminable as she sat on the edge of the bed and listened to the gaming and laughter in the main hall. She'd brought some mending to work on while she waited, but she couldn't sit still.

Just when she worried he may have gone into town with Sitric and some of the men, the door opened and Cormac stopped dead when he spotted her. He shot a quick glance over his shoulder before stepping in and closing the door behind him.

His sea-blue eyes took in the repositioned table and the game board before lifting to meet Astrid's stare. With a sigh of resignation, he strode to the bed and sat on the edge nearest the other side of the little table. "I'm not doing this every night."

"You're doing it until I'm certain you can win."

His lips tightened into a wicked smirk. "I can win already." He picked up one of the white wooden warriors from the edge of the board and moved it toward the king in the center.

"You know how to play?" She moved one of the black pieces to better defend the king, her hopes sinking like a rotten longship.

"Have you already forgotten that both your cousins live with us? Dallan and Eva have boards of their own. And Finn and his sister are the children of an Ostman, both of whom live with our number as well."

"It never occurred to me that they had brought their boards with them," she grumbled. So much for thrashing him. "That's just as well. It gives us more time for you to practice other skills."

In his next two moves, he'd forced her to place one of her warriors into a vulnerable position.

"What other skills will I need?" He didn't look up from the board, making his next move as he spoke.

"Many." She countered his move. "Most of which I doubt you have." She provoked him deliberately, trying to break his concentrated attack on her king. Cormac was trouncing her.

"If you doubt my skills, then why beg for my aid?"

"Beg!" Astrid screeched in protest. Remembering that she sat in a man's room in secret, she lowered her voice to continue berating his poor word choice. "I do not *beg*. You were fortunate that I offered you any sort of truce in the first place."

"Which reminds me," he added smoothly, as though she hadn't just lost her temper. "Have you spoken with your brother?"

Astrid tsked at him, as much to buy her time to contemplate her next move in the game as to forestall the conversation. "Of course I spoke with my brother."

Cormac narrowed his eyes. "About choosing Sláine as his bride?"

"If I change my mind overnight, he'll be suspicious. We have weeks. Let it sit for a while and then I'll pretend I've gotten to know her better."

"Or you could actually get to know her better." His men advanced again, surrounding her king and claiming the victory.

Frowning, Astrid reset the board. Though he'd convinced her that he could play the game, she liked having something to occupy them while they spoke. She took the first turn this time, moving one of the white pieces along the edge toward his king.

He responded with an oddly offensive maneuver for someone defending.

"You still haven't told me anything of these games," he pointed out, waiting as she took her turn.

Astrid swallowed, her anger faltering. She needed to tell him that he had to get Sitric's permission to compete, but she knew he wouldn't like that one bit. As much as she disliked working with him, she really did need his cooperation. Not quite ready to take that risk, she answered his initial question instead.

"They test skills that we value in a man. Many deal with water." Astrid's gaze lifted as a thought struck her. "Do you even know how to swim?" If he didn't, he'd surely be killed.

The hint of a smile lifted the corners of his lips. "I know how to swim," he whispered with amusement.

"It's not just swimming. It's fighting in the water. They'll try to drown you."

"Careful, my lady. You almost sound concerned for my welfare."

Astrid felt her cheeks warm as her anger returned. "If you die, my plan will fail." It sounded cold even to her ears, but the last thing she needed was to develop any sort of feelings for the warrior in all of this. That would ruin far more than just her plan for the games. And she still hadn't forgotten that this was entirely his fault. The least he could do was help her out of the situation he'd created. "There will be rowing as well, maybe sailing. Have you ever been on a boat?"

"I sailed with your brother not two moons ago," he replied, his voice unnervingly calm.

It had become something of a game to Astrid since the warrior had come to Dyflin—trying to get him to argue back. She'd nearly succeeded once, had seen the fire ignite behind his eyes, but his tone had stayed as calm then as it did now. His unnatural calm concerned her, for how could a man live a true life if he never gave himself over to his emotions now and again?

"There will also be drinking contests." She leveled a doubtful look at him.

"I drink with the men every night after dinner."

"Aye, but you'll be deep in your cups for the contest. And you just don't seem like the type. Have you ever even *been* drunk?" she prodded.

"Have you ever considered that mayhap I'm drunk every night, but I'm quiet enough you can't tell?"

She hadn't, but she was now. It didn't matter, so long as he could hold his own in the contest, yet her curiosity got the better of her. "Are you?"

He shrugged. "Sometimes."

Taking her next move, Astrid sighed. "Men *die* in the contests, Cormac. I need to be certain you understand that you must take this seriously or your life could be in danger."

"It's touching that you're so worried for my safety, but I assure you, I'm familiar with the concept of a violent competition." As if to drive home the point, he captured one of her men on the board.

A fluttering traveled through her chest as her heartbeat picked up Lifting one of her game pieces, she rolled it around in her fingers as she decided on her next move.

As much as she wanted to continue prodding him—and he'd handed her an excellent opportunity to do just that—she really needed to get the most difficult part of the conversation out of the way before they planned any further.

"Sitric told me something today that is going to complicate our plan," she began, trying to use some tact instead of simply unleashing her temper. "All the men competing will be men he has chosen and invited, so that he is happy with whomever wins my hand."

Beside her, Cormac's arm stilled mid-reach for the board. "Then how do you plan to get me into the competition at all?"

"You'll have to convince him." She took a deep breath, bracing herself.

CHAPTER EIGHT

ORMAC SET DOWN the playing piece he held, completing his move while Astrid's words sank in.

"Let me get this straight," he replied, turning to take in her response. "Not only do you wish me to risk my life to save you from an undesired marriage, but now I also have to beg your brother for the opportunity to do so?"

He should never have agreed to this bargain. Sitting back, away from their game, Cormac crossed his arms and regarded Astrid for the second time since he'd entered his room to find her waiting.

The first time he'd focused on her fully, he realized that when she wasn't thwarting his every move she was—in point of fact— the most beautiful woman he'd ever seen. During their previous encounters, he'd been so distracted by her temper that he hadn't noticed the flecks of gold in her fiery hair and her honey-hued eyes.

Or the spray of freckles that spread over the bridge of her nose.

Or the way that her lips resembled a boat instead of a bow.

It had been all of a moment's time before Cormac realized that he needed to focus entirely on the game before he somehow managed to convince himself that he was attracted to the infuriating woman. Lord knows that of all the women in all the world, Astrid was the last one he'd want to be trapped in a home with—her and her sharp tongue.

But though his mind and heart knew well the dangers, his body seemed to have other ideas. So he did the only reasonable thing: he did not repeat the mistake of looking at her again.

At least until her final, most ridiculous statement, when shock conquered his good sense.

"First, you are risking your life to preserve your honor after forcing a lady into a marriage against her will. Second, if you are unwilling to speak with him, then don't." She flipped a long, red tendril of hair over her shoulder. "We can go right back to the way things were, and even though I may not be able to escape my marriage, I will do everything in my power to thwart my brother's."

"You won't have to beg him, though," she added. "As I said before, you're a prince and a Gael and a warrior of great renown, with connections to Brian, even. If you asked him to call off the tournament and give you my hand he'd probably do it."

"You know I cannot," Cormac reminded her.

"Yes, yes," she waved a hand. "Your oath forbids it, I remember. But my point is that if you simply *ask* him to allow you to compete, I can't imagine he would deny you."

Cormac didn't understand her plan, but he wasn't certain she did, either. She'd have to marry eventually, and why putting it off another few months mattered he hadn't a clue.

"I understand why you would wish to be selective in your choice of a husband, but I don't see why marrying a Gael would be so terrible."

"A Gael would not understand why we sacrifice to Odin, why we welcome an honorable death. I will not watch my identity suffocate in the arms of a man who would see me assimilate. I will not raise my children as anything other than Ostmen. And I will not leave Dyflin unless I go to another settlement where the laws of my people are the laws of that land."

She'd gone breathless by the end of her impassioned speech, her face flushed and her hands in defiant fists at her side.

Gormla's words came back to him then, that Astrid acted

most often from a place of fear. A fact that had never been clearer to him than it was now, in her poorly hatched plan to cling to the life she had instead of the one for which she was destined.

Cormac had taken a total of four oaths when he joined the Fianna, one of them being that he would marry for love. Another was that he would always offer aid to those in need of it, so long as they weren't doing wrong.

Astrid may not be following the course of action he would recommend, but she wasn't in the wrong, either. And she had made a valid point in their earlier conversation—he was directly responsible for her current plight, though he doubted she'd have avoided it much longer without his interference.

"Ask me to help you, and I cannot refuse."

Her brows furrowed. "I've already asked you."

"You demanded recompense for a perceived slight, proposed a truce, and then explained what you wanted. You never actually asked for my help."

"You agreed, nonetheless," she argued. "Why must I ask now?"

"Because this scheme of yours grows wilder by the day, and I'm starting to feel that perhaps the terms aren't as equitable as I initially believed. But," he held up a hand to stop her from interrupting, "if someone is in need of my help, I must offer it."

"Why?"

"It was another of my oaths."

"Odin's arse, how many of those did you make?"

"Four."

She worried her bottom lip, picking up one of her game pieces and twirling it in her fingers anxiously, as she'd done earlier. Setting it down loudly, she turned to him.

"Will you please help me escape a marriage against my will?" She choked on the word 'please,' but she managed to get it out.

"Happily," he grumbled. Now he was well and truly mixed up in their family's affairs.

They played out the next few turns of the game in silence,

before Cormac realized yet another potential problem.

"If you expect Sitric to believe I wish to wed you, you'll have to stop yelling at me. At least in front of him," he added, holding in a laugh at the horrified look on her face.

"If I'm too nice to you, he'll suspect something," she countered. "I think it's better to continue with the yelling."

Aye, that sounded about right.

But her response wasn't tinged with its usual bite. Likely she'd disagree with him for argument's sake, but heed his advice anyway. How else would she continue vexing him?

THE FOLLOWING MORN, Cormac sought out Illadan, the leader of the Fianna, to let him in on the events of the past two days. Illadan stood in the light misting of rain, awaiting the arrival of the rest of the Fianna. They met every morn in the field outside the hall to go on a run around Dyflin together through the muddy peat bogs before running drills.

Beside him stood Broccan, the commander of Brian's men who had asked to be reassigned to the Fianna. Illadan had a temperament akin to Brian's—loyal to a fault, lethal to his enemies, and a bit of a romantic at heart. Broccan was both loyal and lethal, but not once in the years after his wife's death had Cormac seen him smile.

He greeted the two men, childhood friends turned brothers-in-arms.

"You look grimmer than usual," Illadan remarked.

"I've made what is, in all likelihood, a terrible decision," Cormac muttered, feeling more empathy than usual with the grumpy Broccan. "I thought I should tell you what was actually going on, since it will look even stranger from the outside."

"Did you kill someone?" Broccan asked.

"I've made a bargain with Astrid."

Illadan's amused grin spread ear-to-ear. Broccan rolled his eyes.

"She's going to convince Sitric to marry Sláine instead of

doing her best to undermine us."

"And…" Illadan prompted.

"And I'm going to compete in the games, win, and then help her somehow escape marriage." He threw his hands up. "Her plan isn't terribly clear to me, but she believes it will work. I came to ask your leave to seek out Sitric this morning and discuss it with him."

"You know you can't marry her," Broccan interrupted.

"She assures me that it won't come to that," Cormac replied.

"You have my permission to miss training today, on the condition that you relay, in precise detail, how your conversation with Sitric goes." Illadan appeared barely able to contain himself at the thought of Cormac competing for the hand of the woman he couldn't stand.

The irony wasn't lost on him, either. He just didn't find it particularly funny at the moment.

It didn't take Cormac long to track down Sitric, who sat in the family's hall, breaking his fast with Gormla and Astrid.

"Cormac!" Sitric shouted the greeting as soon as Cormac strode into the hall. "Come, join us!"

Sitric was so like his youngest brother, Diarmid. Loud, warm, and exuberant, both Cormac's brother and the Ostman king had no shortage of hospitality. Cormac had always craved the quiet, preferring to take in his surroundings and keep to himself.

He approached the trio, seated at the far end of the center table, but did not sit. "I had hoped to speak with you in private when you had a moment," Cormac told him, using a great deal of restraint not to glance sideways at Astrid. The last thing he needed was the princess accusing him of making a mess of this on purpose.

"I share most business matters with these two lovely ladies," Sitric grinned. "If it's something they'll learn about anyway, we can discuss while we eat."

Cormac considered how best to ask for a private audience, when Astrid caught his attention by making a face at him.

Squeezing her lips together emphatically, she nodded once in the direction of her brother.

Apparently, she saw no problem with doing this publicly, so Cormac pressed on. Or, perhaps she was using public humiliation as part of his penance.

"I wish to compete in the *leikmót*."

Sitric stopped chewing, setting down the bread he'd been about to bite. "You wish to marry my sister?"

Reminding himself he must convince Sitric of the earnestness of his request, he managed to keep all sarcasm from his response. "Aye."

Gormla eyed him suspiciously over the rim of her cup. Astrid's face flushed like a ripe apple. Her pale complexion did her no favors in concealing her thoughts.

"I had no idea." Sitric sat up straighter, turning to his sister then back to Cormac. "We've not yet sent the runners. If you wish it, you can simply marry her. I know you to be the best sort of man, and you are of an equal status with her."

After Astrid's comment last night, Cormac anticipated such a suggestion from the magnanimous king. "I don't believe she's fond of me," he replied, "and I won't force a woman into marriage. The games will afford me the opportunity to win her goodwill by proving that I value the same things she does."

"And what might those things be?" Astrid asked, playing her part well.

"Courage, honor, wit, and an understanding and acceptance of the Ostman ways. I admit, I have much to learn yet, but I would like the opportunity to try."

"What say you, sister? Shall we humor our esteemed guest?"

Astrid narrowed her eyes at him, but Cormac saw the glimmer in them. She found the entire ordeal amusing. Her fingers rapped over the oaken tabletop, as though she were deep in thought. Then, with a telling curve at the corner of her full lips, she gave her answer.

"Aye. I'll be impressed if he lives through it, let alone wins it."

"There you have it," Sitric proclaimed happily. "We'll begin in a fortnight, though you're welcome to begin training with my men as you please."

Cormac offered his thanks, but instead of feeling relieved that their ploy had worked so well, he grew more concerned that this was a mistake.

A very dangerous mistake.

CHAPTER NINE

T HE NEXT FEW days kept Astrid too busy to meet with Cormac. She and her mother spent dawn till dusk scraping together enough workers and materials to build temporary houses for their influx of guests. After dinner, she collapsed onto her bed in an exhausted pile of stress and worry. If she didn't start preparing Cormac, he wouldn't have any real advantage over the men who arrived in ten days.

Five days after Cormac interrupted their breakfast with his shockingly thoughtful speech, Astrid decided that no matter how tired she felt, she would go to his room and start teaching him the rules and expectations of the games. But that was hours from now.

At present, Astrid sat at the table in the hall with ledgers spread and a pile of counting stones.

"Alright," she rubbed her throbbing temples. "If he's invited fifteen men, and they each bring at least two companions, we'll need to feed an additional forty-five mouths for over a month."

"I'm far less concerned over the food than I am the ale," her mother remarked, shuffling the papers until she found the one she wanted. "Our next shipment won't arrive for weeks, and I've only been buying enough for the household and our guests."

"But the ale's the most important thing!" Astrid grabbed the parchment from her mother, as though staring at the numbers herself might alter them. "Sitric will kill us if we run out of ale."

"Oh, I'm well aware, dear. And that's just the beginning of

our logistical problems. Even working as we've been, I'm concerned it's too much for just the two of us."

That gave Astrid an idea. Cormac's wry comment from nearly a sennight ago—that perhaps she should get to know Sláine better—had been bouncing guiltily through her mind ever since. She hated that he had been the one to suggest it, but it was a good point nonetheless.

"What?" her mother asked, clearly sensing the shift in her mood.

"We could ask Catrin and Sláine to help," she suggested. "It would alleviate some of our problems and give us the opportunity to see how they handle household responsibilities."

In response, Gormla called Bodil, the nearest serving girl, over to her. "Find the princesses and ask them to join us here," she ordered.

As Bodil hurried off to do her mistress's bidding, Astrid set down the ledger. "Alehouses," she thought aloud. "We could use the alehouses. They never run out."

"Yes!" Gormla agreed, pointing at her with a grin. "Hurry down there now and ask about their stores. We can discuss precise measures when you return."

"Why me?" Astrid protested, standing anyway.

"You're younger and faster," Gormla answered. "I'll start in on the meals while you're gone."

Without another word of argument, Astrid left the hall and headed down the hill into Dyflin toward the alehouse. News of the coming tournament already buzzed about the town around her, palpable excitement tinged the air. As she walked, however, the reality of her situation sank in further with every step.

They were ordering food.

She was securing a steady supply of ale at this very moment.

This tournament was really happening, and that meant that she would really be married, unless she finally got a plan into place aside from simply refusing the marriage.

It wasn't that she hadn't thought about it, she certainly had.

Night and day, she'd contemplated just how she could get out of this ordeal, but no answers had come. For the first time in her memory, Astrid couldn't solve a problem. And that, in and of itself, posed an entirely different sort of problem.

Perhaps it was because this particular problem was so close to her. Not only was marriage deeply personal, but it also held far-reaching consequences that would determine the course of her life.

Some of her ideas had potential, but the strategies of them yet eluded her. Some of them were as far-fetched as the notion of marrying anyone but a fellow Ostman had once been. One of her favorite ideas had been simply getting on a ship herself and sailing far north in search of her sister. It had been many years since Gytha had married the King of Noregr and left for the northern reaches of the world.

Since the day Astrid had learned of her sister's betrothal all those years ago, she'd been envious, and she had decided that she, too, would marry an Ostman and join her sister in Noregr. That her brother didn't understand her desire, would not even entertain it, was slowly breaking her heart. And without her heart working toward her problem, it felt an insurmountable challenge. For all her life, he'd been her unshakeable ally, her supporter in the face of all her problems. But now he was the one creating those problems for her.

Another, deeper fear in the back of her mind, was the possibility that she could end up akin to her dear cousin Eva, who had been traded as a hostage following the battle they lost to Brian last winter. Astrid knew well the isolation Eva suffered, and her cousin was not even an Ostman. Eva was a daughter of Éire from a long line of Gaelic kings and princes. Though Eva embraced and enjoyed Astrid's heritage, she was shunned as an outcast solely for having been on the losing side of the battle. It was not a stretch for Astrid to imagine herself in a similar situation, but instead of a hostage of war, she was the hostage of a marriage.

Long before Astrid reached the alehouse, she saw from a

distance the lowest plain at the foot of the city. It was one of the few plains surrounding Dyflin that didn't regularly flood, and was not constantly a mucky bog. Instead of a field of swaying grasses and wildflowers, a flurry of activity filled the space. Countless men carried piles of lumber into the clearing, while others converted them into planks for building.

Even in the cool mists of winter, the men worked so hard that many wore a shirt with no tunic or cloak. She watched them as she descended the hill from her homestead, amazed that construction had already begun so soon after the orders were given. Cormac and the other Fianna worked among them, drawing her attention. Without giving it much thought, Astrid veered from her course toward the alehouse, taking a narrow path that led straight out of town through the side gate and toward the field where the men worked.

Cormac caught sight of her as she strode across the field toward him. Looking askance between his men, who had not yet seemed to notice her, he walked over to meet her.

"Can I help you, princess?"

"I was just surprised to find the Fianna doing anything other than their usual routine." And also now questioning why she had even come out here. She hadn't much to say really.

"We heard you were in need of help, and so we offered it. And it serves as an adequate honing of our strength and skills."

"Well, thank you," she replied awkwardly. What on earth was wrong with her? She shifted uncomfortably, realizing that this was probably the moment to take her leave.

Before she could do so, Cormac took one step closer lowering his voice. "Are you alright?" he asked. "You seem…less intense than usual."

Astrid regarded him with suspicion. "Why are you being nice to me?"

"You have yet to attack, so I have no reason to defend. I'm actually quite a nice person, you know."

"Nice people don't have to tell you that." She resisted the

urge to smile at her jab. It irritated her how much she enjoyed sparring with him.

He crossed his arms over his chest, the impressive amount of muscle drawing her attention for a moment too long. She was grateful he didn't tease her about it—most other men certainly would have.

"Is there something I can help you with?" he tried again.

She frowned, grasping for any sort of reason to have sought him out. "I still haven't figured out a solution to my problem of avoiding marrying you."

"You know, coming from just about anyone else, that would really hurt."

"I think you're right, that I need a plan to avoid my brother just forcing the next-in-line onto me if you refuse," she grumbled. "If I don't come up with something, he's going to foist one of them onto me."

"Perhaps that's the solution, then," Cormac mused, rubbing his chin thoughtfully and squinting into the distance. He kept his dark beard much shorter than most men, hardly longer than the sharp edges of his face.

"Letting him destroy my future?"

"Giving him a reason not to," he corrected gently. "You've told me what you don't want in a husband. You've rejected countless options he's offered you. Try giving him the names of men you *would* marry, just as you suggested he do with Brian."

"That's—" Astrid caught herself mid-denial, "actually not a terrible idea."

He shrugged, drawing her attention once more to his impressive stature. "It's worth trying, at least."

Indeed, it was. And even if that didn't work, it gave Astrid a different perspective on the problem. "Thank you."

"My pleasure, princess."

A tendril of heat threaded through her at the intimate tone of his voice, at the way he caressed the words. She took several steps away, putting distance between them. "I should get to the alehouse."

He smiled at her—which did nothing to quell her alarming reaction to him—and returned to carrying the heavy timber beams.

Cormac was, perhaps, not as devious as she'd believed. Maybe he wasn't always out to ruin her family. And, she grudgingly admitted, he'd been rather helpful just now. But he was a Gaelic prince, sworn to her enemy Brian. Even if he wasn't the worst man to marry—which she still hadn't decided yet—she couldn't actually marry *him*. She'd live the rest of her days surrounded by folk who despised her and her culture.

Maybe he wasn't awful, but he certainly wasn't for her.

ASTRID RETURNED FROM the alehouse before dinner, surprised at just how much ale Maeve had in stock. It would cost a fortune to keep everyone well-watered for a month, but it was possible at least. The moment she returned, Astrid tracked down Sitric. She didn't want to wait to put Cormac's idea into action.

She found him in the hall, meeting with his warriors to determine the games and rules for the tournament.

"I have a solution," she announced.

"Do I have a problem?" Sitric asked.

"What if I choose three men that I would wish to marry? Perhaps we could find some common ground—"

His cheeks tightened in a way that told Astrid he wasn't in agreement with her new plan. "I've already invited everyone who is to compete." He sighed. "I'm sorry, Astrid. The competition will decide the marriage. But perhaps the results will be to your liking."

Astrid bit her tongue to keep from arguing. It was clear his mind was made up, and there was no use continuing to walk down that particular path. Normally, Astrid would've panicked.

But this time she wasn't walking alone.

CHAPTER TEN

THE NEXT TEN days flew by in a whirlwind of cutting, sawing, and laying boards to construct the temporary housing necessary to fit the many suitors soon headed their way. Cormac tried not to think overmuch on what would follow after the housing was finished. He didn't know how he felt about any of it, aside from conflicted. Seemingly overnight, Astrid had gone from someone he avoided at all costs to someone who stole the majority of his thoughts.

Many times over those long days of building he contemplated how he might break the news to the rest of the Fianna, to his brothers, that he would be competing for Astrid's hand in marriage. Though he knew an explanation of his plan would quickly dissolve any argument they might have, or even any jesting at his odd shift in allegiance, he still felt that he hadn't found the right words. It was a good plan—he was convinced of that—but something inside him gnawed at him throughout those long days of manual labor.

As the first contestants started trickling into Dyflin, Cormac accepted that the time had come to inform his brothers, and then the rest of the Fianna, of his decision to compete. After dinner in Sitric's hall one day before the games began, Cormac took his brothers to the alehouse in the heart of Dyflin—an occurrence so unusual that they cast him sidelong glances the entire way.

They found the alehouse busier than usual, with both the indoor and outdoor tables stuffed to overflowing, no doubt on account of the impending tournament. Diarmid, turning on his notorious charm, approached Maeve, the establishment's owner with whom he'd become well-acquainted in the course of their time in Dyflin. Cormac didn't even overhear what was said, but following a few brief words, they were seated in the far back corner inside the alehouse, quite near to the bar itself.

"Are you going to tell us why you brought us here?" his middle brother, Conan, asked as Maeve brought their first round of ale.

"Is it that odd for me to want to spend a night out with my brothers after weeks of hard work?" Even Cormac wasn't convinced at the tone in his own voice.

"You rarely leave Sitric's estate," Diarmid replied, "and when you do it's only because we force you."

"True, true," Cormac conceded, though he wasn't able to smile with his admission as he normally would. "The truth is, I've brought you here to tell you something, and I had hoped that copious amounts of ale and the promise of an evening out might hinder any untoward comments."

"Well, you shouldn't have told us that," Diarmid laughed, taking a swig of ale. "Now I'm obligated to go out of my way just to make said comments."

Conan shoved Diarmid, making his ale slosh out of the mug. "Out with it," Conan demanded. "I'll make sure he's not too hard on you, though I can't imagine what our responsible older brother could possibly have done that he believes merits commentary from us heathens."

"After great consideration, I have made the decision to enter into the tournament."

For a long moment, his brothers stared at him blankly, as though unable to comprehend what he'd said.

"You mean in the tournament here?" Conan asked, his grey-blue eyes wide with skepticism.

"The very same, but before you make any wild assumptions, let me explain my plan." He didn't get much farther than that before the pair of them burst into laughter.

"You're going to compete for the hand of the woman who drives you absolutely mad?" Conan sputtered.

"It's because he's secretly in love with her," Diarmid teased. "That's how they get you. First they irritate you, then they ensnare you."

"Shall I tell Cara your views on the matter, then?" Cormac prodded his brother, knowing full well Diarmid's new betrothed would have a thing or two to say over it.

"I'm certain it wouldn't surprise her," Diarmid chuckled, "but I'd appreciate it if you told it in the context of this story."

"So what's really going on then?" Conan asked.

Though both Cormac's brothers were lighter of spirit and wilder than Cormac ever had been, Conan was the more thoughtful of the two, and the more likely to see the truth behind Cormac's statement.

"She approached me about it," Cormac explained, "and offered a truce. If I help her get out of a marriage entirely, in return she will convince Sitric to marry Sláine."

"How is competing going to save her from a marriage?" Conan asked.

Diarmid took it in an entirely different direction, instead, staring pointedly at Cormac with his piercing chestnut gaze and setting down his ale. "You're not actually interested in her, are you?"

Cormac choked on his next swig of ale. "Not in the least," he assured his brother. "It was simply the easiest way to get her out of the way so that we could accomplish our mission."

"Alright," Diarmid allowed hesitantly, "but I think it's a terrible idea."

"How is it a terrible idea?" Cormac asked. "I thought it through, and the only thing that could possibly go wrong would be Sitric—" he paused.

"Forcing you to actually marry her and thus break your oath to Brian?" Conan finished for him.

"Aye," Cormac allowed, "but I'd be willing to anger Sitric if it meant keeping my oath to Brian. I won't be marrying her, no matter how this turns out, but I'm going to do my best to set her up to marry someone of her choosing."

"What does that even mean?" Conan asked. "Are you going to help some other man win if she says she wants to marry him instead?"

"If that's what it comes to, yes," Cormac told him. "I can't marry her, so if she finds someone she would actually like to marry, I'll happily help him on his way to victory. I'll even put in a good word for him with Sitric along the way." It was the least he could do after his questions caused all this in the first place.

After several more rounds of questioning, his brothers grudgingly agreed that it was, in fact, an acceptable plan. Three refills later, Diarmid got his attention once more.

"Do you have any idea who else might be coming?" he asked. "Has Astrid told you who's competing?"

"I've not spoken with her much since we came to our agreement," Cormac responded. "We've both been busy getting ready for the tournament, but as I understand it Sitric invited about a dozen or so men to compete. I had to ask him to include me."

"Well, you should have told us sooner," Conan grumbled, "then we could have given you all of our excellent advice so you had enough time to use it."

Cormac smiled at his brothers, wondering why he had waited so long to talk to them about it. He was so used to them making light of everything and turning life into one great jest that he hadn't really thought of them as fonts of wisdom or sage advice. He made a note not to underestimate them the same way in the future.

All his life he'd been the one looking out for them. He'd happily carried the weight of that responsibility, especially as he knew it was his fault they'd been disowned by their father. Perhaps it was time for Cormac to start focusing more on his own goals and less on raising his brothers. They were grown men now, Fianna warriors in their own right.

And it wasn't that he had raised them entirely on his own, either. Brian had been as a father to them since the day of his sister's wedding. But Cormac knew that the fault of their poor relationship with their family lay entirely with him, and that was no small burden to carry. The least he could do was to help them every step of the way.

The rest of their evening passed in jovial conversation and outrageous betting on who had been invited to compete in the games and whether or not they would show up. Nearing midnight, Cormac stood and ushered his brothers out the door of the alehouse and back up toward Sitric's holding. Tomorrow the games began, and Cormac knew that what he needed more than anything else was a good night's sleep.

THE FOLLOWING MORN started with a bang. Moments after he woke, a clattering sounded outside his bedroom window. Cormac flew from his bed to find all of the Fianna beneath his window, shouting at him and cheering for him to come out.

He couldn't help but roll his eyes. He should've known they'd cause a scene. He knew it was all in good fun, but the attention put every nerve on edge until they frayed into a thousand tiny flames, his skin burning like a Lughnasadh bonfire. Sighing in resignation, he put on his clothes and fortified himself. Not for the day of friendly competition, but for the onslaught of support he knew he would get from his friends. He went out to join them, grabbing a couple of oat cakes on his way through the hall.

They shouted and called to him as he met them in the court-yard, laughter and cheering and a good dose of slapping him on the back following his every step.

"You're going to crush them all," Conan assured him with a smack on his shoulder.

"If you need any help with the rules, come to us," Finn told him, motioning to himself and Dallan, who were both well-versed in the Ostman games.

"We'll be right there if you need us, shouting so loud that your opponents won't be able to think straight," Diarmid promised with a dimpled grin.

Cormac didn't doubt it, thanking them as they walked together down to the tournament field on the outskirts of Dyflin. In spite of the late night out with his brothers, he felt ready to take on whatever challenges came his way. He wasn't worried over his opponents, but instead was curious about what men would be competing against him.

The temporary housing that they had helped build bustled with activity. Families had already arrived and buzzed like bees about a hive as they settled into the four small halls, unloading carts and unpacking horses. Cormac didn't recognize any of the men he saw carrying their belongings into whichever hall they'd been assigned. Astrid and her mother stood in their midst like trees in a storm, directing everyone to the appropriate rooms.

Sitric greeted each guest with huge hugs for which he was known. It amused Cormac to no end to watch how everyone reacted when the giant of a king charged them, arms wide, as though he were going to squeeze the life from them.

"Cormac!" Sitric bellowed from across the field, waving him over with a beaming smile. When they came within earshot and arms' reach, Sitric pulled Cormac into an enthusiastic hug, of the sort he'd given every single person that morn. "The man who wishes to wed my sister! Well, one of them, anyway," he chuckled.

Cormac slipped a sidelong glance at Astrid, who stood but a few feet away with Gormla. She narrowed her eyes at her brother. "You shouldn't prod him," she chastised. "His pride will be bruised enough in the coming games."

"I doubt that," Diarmid championed, stepping forward beside Cormac. "He's going to beat every single one of them."

Long before the sun rose to its zenith, all of the men Sitric invited seated themselves around the field to listen to several of

Sitric's men instruct them on the rules of the day's game. *Knattleikr*, they called it, though that meant naught to him. As far as Cormac could tell, it was a game of wrestling that somehow involved a ball and a wooden stick. Two of Sitric's men demonstrated the game briefly, but it did little to convince Cormac that the ball and stick were necessary at all to the game.

All the men stood, preparing to take sides against one another. Astrid and Gormla, along with much of Sitric's household, sat along the edge of the field to watch the opening match of the games. Sitric's men handed out long wooden sticks, as thick as a woman's arm and twice as long. Cormac allowed himself one swift glance at Astrid, who gave him the slightest hint of a smile and a nod indicating her support. His friends, on the other hand, shouted so loudly that Cormac could hardly hear his own thoughts.

The sixteen competitors paired up, throwing stones to determine which men were of comparable strength. Cormac was paired with a man a hair shorter than him but just as broad. Tall, with sandy blonde hair that reminded Cormac of Finn's, the man clearly knew his way around a sword. They stood about ten yards apart, his opponent holding the stick and preparing to hit the ball to him when another group of horses rode into the settlement. Perhaps he'd misunderstood Astrid when she said fifteen men were invited. Or perhaps Sitric had later invited another competitor. The men around Cormac were entirely focused on the game; not one seemed to notice.

Cormac's attention was divided between the game and the horses. He couldn't quite make out the features of the men, but he could tell there were no women with them. Astrid rose, presumably to greet the newcomers, but something about the entire situation felt wrong, setting the hairs on the back of his neck on end.

Sitric's men began the count. His opponent raised the stick, drawing Cormac's attention sharply back to the game at hand. And at the same moment that the stick cracked against the ball,

Cormac heard a sound that he'd hoped never to hear again. His stomach dropped as he caught the ball.

And his father's voice rang out across the field.

CHAPTER ELEVEN

ASTRID'S IRRITATION FLARED as she watched a group of horses stop behind their seats at the edge of the field nearest the housing.

"Did you invite someone else?" Astrid asked Sitric under her breath.

"No," he answered. "No one else should be here."

"Then who is that?" She motioned with her head toward the men now dismounting.

Sitric turned, his pale brow furrowing. "That looks—it can't be."

"Who? It can't be *who*?" she demanded again.

"It looks like the King of Connachta." Sitric nudged their mother beside him, turning her attention also to the man walking toward them. "I've only seen him once, but I recall he had the same scar over his left brow."

"Why is he here?"

He shrugged, turning back to check the progress of the game in front of them. "He shouldn't be. He knows he's not welcome after the battle last winter."

If her brother guessed correctly and the man was, indeed, the King of Connachta, he'd been one of the kings who fought alongside Brian to defeat her brother and sack Dyflin. Though the man's alliance with Brian had been temporary, the damage to her opinion of him was permanent.

Astrid rose with a huff to greet the guests. She needed to pay attention to Cormac's performance in this match in order to offer advice and insight on his opponents and how he might beat them in the next challenge. In the few minutes Astrid had seen, Cormac appeared distracted and confused, which surprised her. By all accounts he was a man of great skill and athleticism, and such a game should be easy for him.

Concern over her choice of champion threaded her thoughts as she went to discover the identity of this uninvited guest. Her mother and her brother followed on her heels, both seeming as irritated as she felt.

"Greetings, great King Sitric of the Ostmen of Dyflin," the man with a scarred brow called.

"I'm afraid you have me at a disadvantage," Sitric replied, his signature grin nowhere in sight, "for I am not privy to your name and title."

"It's been many years and you were but a boy when last we looked upon one another," the man said gruffly. "I am Cahill, King of Connachta, and this is my eldest son, Teague, my successor. I wish for him to compete in your games, that he might win the hand of your sister and our two great kingdoms can unite."

Her brother went on to reply, but Astrid missed most of what he said when her mother nudged her from behind. Astrid turned her head ever so slightly as her mother whispered in her ear.

"Cahill is an enemy of Brian still," she told Astrid. "He would ally with us when we rebel again. Teague might not be a terrible choice of husband for you."

Astrid nodded her understanding, but did not much care for that insight. The thought of marrying a man who'd attacked Dyflin barely a year ago felt as much a betrayal of her people as marrying a Gael—and Teague was both. Though, she realized with horror, Cormac and his brothers had likely numbered among Brian's men in the battle. Allegiances on this island shifted like the winds.

It took her several moments of not really listening to the

conversation to reach a second, equally unwelcome realization of Cahill. If Cahill was the king of Connachta, and Cormac and his brothers were princes of Connachta, then this must be their father and brother.

Perhaps that was why he'd been so distracted. Maybe he'd caught sight of them just as the game began. That must be it, she decided, unwilling to believe anything else could cause trouble for her champion. The thought that Cormac would be competing against his own brother, and that she could potentially end up marrying Teague instead of Cormac made her squirm in discomfort. She didn't like that one bit.

The more she considered it, the more she realized that yet another factor tallied against Teague as a potential husband: the location of his kingdom, deep in the heart of Gaelic Éire. There were no nearby Ostman settlements. She would have virtually no contact with her own people. In the Kingdom of Connachta, Astrid would be in complete and utter isolation, and likely unwelcome.

"We'd be happy to have you join us," she heard her brother say when she finally turned her attention back to the conversation with the king. "Please, this way."

Cahill must have said something important and convincing for her brother to change his manner so swiftly, and to welcome to the contest a man who'd battled against them so recently. Once again, her brother proved himself too kind a soul to be king. Astrid would've turned the lout out before he could draw breath.

Sitric called one of his men to go and join the game alongside Teague, so that the numbers were still even on each team. In Astrid's mind, it mattered nearly as little as the teams themselves. The game was more a test of each man's individual strength more than it was any sort of effort at unity.

With the business of the uninvited guest settled, Astrid returned with her mother and brother to their seats atop small wooden chairs on the side of the field of play. Most of the household had come down out of the holding to watch the first match of the tournament. The game tested strength and stamina, a method to measure each man on his own amidst chaos, and lasted until Sitric called a halt. Not knowing when the match ended would put the men's strength of will to the test as much as their physical might.

Finally able to return her attention to the game, Astrid searched the men to find Cormac so that she could track his performance. Though he wore a loose-fitted tunic, the muscles in his arms swelled even beneath his clothing, and he was one of only a handful of the men on the field with such impressive bulk. Not that she ought to be noticing such things, especially since she wasn't *actually* looking for a husband. Just as her attention settled comfortably back into the game, her brother nudged her with his elbow beside her.

"I wanted to let you know," he told her, "that you have a part to play in all this, aside from helping judge the victor of the competition, of course."

"And what might that be?"

"I need you to set aside time to speak with each man. Your assessment of their characters will be an important part of my decision. In the end, I won't have you saddled with a dishonorable man."

Astrid tore her gaze from the chaos of the field so that she could look at her brother. "Thank you," she whispered, and she meant it. She may not relish the idea of setting aside time to meet with over a dozen different men and assess their characters, especially as she didn't plan to marry any of them, but she appreciated the care in her brother's request.

Assuming he'd finished, she turned yet again back to the game. Cormac hit the ball to his opponent across the field, the only man who matched him in size and strength. The man caught it, and Cormac charged at him down the field to try to wrest it from his grasp.

Astrid scooted to the edge of her seat.

Cormac's shoulder slammed into the man's chest, knocking

him flat on his back with a groan and a thud.

She cheered, her hands raising of their own accord. Beside her, someone cleared their throat. She turned to find her mother and brother both staring at her in confusion and surprise. She shrugged, nodding toward the field.

"It was a good hit."

A cheeky smirk rose on her brother's face, earning him a good smack on the shoulder. He chuckled, and they all returned their attention to the *knattleikr* game. Perhaps he really could win. He was certainly one of the largest of the men and in the best shape by her measure. Maybe he could do it. Maybe he really could win. Astrid certainly hoped so, for her future depended on it.

Astrid fell deeper and deeper into the match—into every sprint, every swing of the bat, every movement across the field— until her awareness was naught but the game itself. In particular, the experience of one specific player on the field. Until, of course, her brother nudged her again. This time the glare she turned to him could have turned a man to stone, but he'd long since become immune to such looks from her. She supposed he thought they were some sort of jest, but she was deadly serious and seriously annoyed. Could she not simply watch the game in peace?

"Yes, brother?"

"I just thought that you might like to know an interesting fact I learned about one of the players." He paused, as though expecting some sort of reaction from her. Realizing that wasn't forthcoming, he continued. "It seems purely by happenstance, I've invited someone who fulfills many of your desires in a husband."

That got her attention. "Oh?"

"Do you see that man?" He pointed to the mess of bodies in the center of the field.

"I see about twenty men, brother. Which do you mean?" It was impossible to tell to whom he pointed.

"The man wrestling Cormac."

The mention of the warrior's name sent a shiver through her—an odd reaction, indeed. She found him then, the tall, broad man with sandy brown hair.

"That man, Cairell, is a prince of the Dál Fiatach. And, just like our mother, is the son of an Ostman slave and a Gaelic king," he explained.

"Really?" That genuinely surprised Astrid. A half-Ostman was much closer to what she wanted in a husband. "That *is* interesting," she admitted.

A sharp intake of breath from everyone along the sidelines alerted Astrid that something exciting must be happening in the match. She and Sitric both turned toward the field. Cormac laid flat on his back, clearly having been knocked over by Cairell. If he didn't get up soon, he'd lose this bout.

Astrid's hands gripped the edge of her seat, squeezing as she leaned forward, as though she could somehow help him solve this dilemma. "Come on," she groaned through gritted teeth.

Cormac moved his legs and his arms, still holding the ball at least, but for how much longer?

Cairell raised his free arm. He was going to slam it down to try to free the ball, she realized.

Astrid's breath caught as she prepared for the impact.

CHAPTER TWELVE

H E NEEDED TO get on top. The game had gone well so far, in spite of his initial distraction by the arrival of his father and brother. But right now his shoulder hurt something fierce after that tackle and a giant held him pinned to the soggy ground.

The man's hand pounded against his chest, where his arms held the ball tight. Pain seared across his middle at the blow, but he didn't drop the ball.

A great, raucous cheer broke out from the sidelines. He didn't need to look. His chest swelled, bolstering him as the Fianna cheered him on, reminding him that he was the best. They were the best.

And that was why they were here, why Astrid had chosen him as her champion.

Throwing his hips sharply upward, he reached his hands over his head, moving fast so the man didn't have time to make a grab at the ball. The motion threw his opponent off-balance, and Cormac took immediate advantage, using his entire body to flip the man onto *his* back.

All Cormac wanted was to finish the game and then disappear somewhere to collect his thoughts alone before he confronted his father and brother. He wasn't ready to speak with them, not yet.

At long last, after hours of playing, Sitric called a halt to the game. Cormac moved off the man he'd just spent much of the day wrestling, offering his arm to help him up.

"Well played," the man congratulated him. "I'll have to remember that little trick next time."

"I thought you had me. Cormac," he introduced himself.

"Cairell," the man replied in kind. "What brings you to the tournament?" He glanced at Astrid, seated beside her brother and watching them intently. "Other than a beautiful wife, that is," he grinned.

Cormac felt his shoulders tense at Cairell's words, but he shook the feeling off. "For me, it's just the wife," he lied. Well, it wasn't precisely a lie. He was here only for Astrid, but to help her get out of a marriage, not wed her himself. "You?"

"An alliance with the wealth of Dyflin would please my father," Cairell replied. "And a marriage to an Ostman princess would please my mother."

"Is your mother an Ostman?" Cormac asked, unsure what to make of that last statement.

Cairell nodded, grinning. "I'm only half a prince," he laughed. "My mother is an Ostman slave. Or was, anyway. She's raised her status since my father took her to wife."

Cormac's blood ran cold. "Does Astrid know that?"

This man could be the answer to all her problems. Cormac should be elated, happy to have solved it for her. Yet here he stood, wanting to go another round with Cairell.

"'Tis no secret," Cairell shrugged. "But I doubt it will upset her overmuch, as her own grandmother was in the same position."

"Of course not," Cormac agreed. "It shouldn't be a problem at all. Best of luck to you."

Cairell grinned. "And to you. I imagine we'll be seeing much of one another over the coming weeks."

"I look forward to it."

The onlookers all rushed the field as one. Some to congratulate, others to see to wounds. For, as Astrid had warned him, this game had indeed been brutal. Most men were bloodied and bruised. A few were wounded enough to need a healer.

Diarmid shouted at him triumphantly, congratulating him

with a grin and a slap on the shoulder that caused another rush of pain. Cormac grimaced, but did his best not to let it show.

"It was thanks to you lot," he told them, finding a smile amidst the chaos of his thoughts and the pain in his shoulder. "I think God himself could hear you shouting at me," he laughed.

"And we'll be doing the same at every match," Conan assured him.

"You played well for your first time," Finn commented. "I have a few suggestions for you, but I've never seen a better comeback."

Cormac allowed himself a moment to soak in the contagious joy of his friends. Darkness overtook his thoughts when he spotted Teague and his father searching the men on the field, as though they were looking for him. Beside him, Illadan's attention went to Cahill and Teague as well.

"Let's leave Cormac to get cleaned up and then we can celebrate properly after the feast," Illadan declared, nodding behind him for Cormac to disappear while he still had time.

Cormac mouthed a thank you, moving quickly away from the tournament field. As they were already outside of Dyflin, the walk to the river was a blessedly short one. Cormac arrived and took off his shoes and shirt, recalling that day in spring so long ago when Diarmid had leapt into the river. Cormac wasn't about to splash around like a flopping fish as his brother had, but he relished the thought of the cool water soothing his aches and bruises from the match.

The appearance of his father and brother perplexed him. Cahill would always be an enemy of Brian, their brief and tepid alliance notwithstanding. That had been purely to halt Sitric's increasingly bold raids inland, and had ended in the same moment as the battle. Cormac doubted Sitric would soon forget that Cahill sided with Brian against Dyflin, no matter how brief.

But Sitric had allowed Cahill to stay and Teague to compete, which could mean but one thing: Cahill must have offered him some support against Brian.

Everyone knew that Sitric had only submitted to Brian after a devastating loss at a bloody battle, the bloodiest Cormac had seen or heard of in his lifetime. No king wanted to be the subject of another king. Cormac would wager that Teague and his father were here to start an alliance against Brian. If Teague won and married Astrid, Sitric would potentially have the strength of both Connachta and Midhe behind him. An alliance such as that might be enough to put an end to Brian's bid for the High Kingship and his goal of uniting all the kingdoms.

As he finished stripping down, Cormac stepped into the icy river. The cold crept up his legs and torso like fingers reaching up from the deep, pulling him in to soak his aching shoulder in the frigid water. He couldn't stay in long, he knew, lest he risk losing all the heat in his body and going into shock, but he needed to stay in long enough to help him recover from the match.

What if his brother won? Cormac had been so certain of his ability to consistently place at the top of the contests of skill, but now that confidence faltered. As children, Teague had always been the stronger, the faster, even the smarter of the two of them. Perhaps it had been due to the age difference, with Teague being his elder by several years. Or, perhaps, Teague was simply better than him.

The crunch of footsteps nearby halted his dark musings. Astrid strode toward him across the flat, grassy bank.

And, for the first time since he spied his brother and father, Cormac's calm returned.

CHAPTER THIRTEEN

ASTRID FROZE. CORMAC'S piercing cerulean gaze pinned her feet in place as he watched her from the river below. The glassy surface of the water looked inviting, but Astrid knew it would be freezing at this time of year. He stood still as a stone, his expression equally intense and unreadable. She'd hoped to catch him before he got in, for she knew that all the men would want to clean themselves of the dirt, mud, and blood they'd accumulated over the course of the matches.

Cormac was always quiet. It was one of the things that initially had irritated her about him, though there were many. But during the match, she noted an unusual shift in his demeanor. He seemed even more intense than usual. And now, as she stood there staring at him, uncertain what to say, she knew that something was wrong.

She swallowed, collecting her thoughts and searching for words. The rippling muscles that covered every inch of his exposed torso distracted her more than she liked. She'd seen plenty of men without their shirts, as her brother's warriors seemed keen to be rid of them when they ran drills in the hot summer months. But for some reason, the sight of this particular man drew her complete attention. A warm sensation swirling up from her belly finally shook her from her trance.

After all that time, Cormac still hadn't said a word to her.

Should she leave? This felt like a mistake. Perhaps he needed more time alone to process whatever was going on with him. He did seem to prefer time apart from everyone else. Astrid noted with some amusement that instead of bothering him to check on him, what he likely wanted was solitude. But if she turned back now, it would only be all the stranger.

"You'll be covered in bruises by morning," she called. There, she hadn't even insulted him.

The hint of a smile lifted the corner of his lips. "You seem awfully concerned about my welfare of late."

Astrid huffed at that, walking further toward the river so that she didn't have to raise her voice to continue the conversation. "You are my champion, after all," she replied tartly. "If I don't take good care of you, how will you win on my behalf?"

His cocky smile deepened, but Cormac said nothing.

"I came to congratulate you on your impressive victory." Damnit, no she hadn't. But the compliment tumbled out all the same.

"Thank you." He cupped his hands, pouring water over his shoulder and rubbing it into his arms to clean off the mud and grime. "Do you have any idea what our next event will be?"

"I don't."

"Do you think you could find out? Though they did a fine job of teaching us the game, it would be nice to be able to prepare ahead of time."

"I'll see what I can learn," she agreed. She couldn't very well expect him to perform his best if she didn't cooperate, odd though it felt not to thwart him. "I can tell you that you will undoubtedly have more matches like this one. Now that everyone knows how to play, my brother can more accurately judge your skill and strength."

He nodded, continuing to wash himself, scrubbing his face in a way that only encouraged the swirling warmth that tugged at Astrid's belly.

"I should work with you more on preparation for other events, but my mother and I have had more to do than we've been able to adequately keep up on."

"I imagine managing so many guests at once, especially in their own halls, is quite an organizational feat."

"It's not only that," Astrid told him, recalling her brother's request. "Sitric informed me during the match that I must meet and speak with every man competing, to make a measure of him. At least I don't need to meet with you," she pointed out her mood lightening a little. "I've spoken with you plenty, and it doesn't matter anyway, as I'm not going to marry any of them."

Cormac stilled, droplets of water falling from his broad shoulders into the river. "Aye, you do," he countered. "I expect the same opportunities to prove myself as the next man. Whatever questions you're asking them, I'll answer the same."

A subtle change overcame his appearance, though Astrid couldn't decide what was actually different. As his arms crossed, the muscles flexed larger and tighter than they had before, as though he were squeezing them in frustration.

"Fine," Astrid agreed, doing her best to aid her chosen champion. She may as well get one interview out of the way. "We can have our time together when you finish washing."

He nodded, and she retreated so that he could finish up and put his clothes back on. When he called her back over, they sat down together beside the river and spent several moments in silence, listening to its gentle gurgling. It meandered just past their feet and a chill fell upon them, the crisp air of a winter evening descending as the sun sank toward the horizon. Night came early this time of the year, and dinner would begin shortly—a grand feast, as Astrid well knew, for she and her mother had planned the entire thing.

She wasn't about to miss it, but she didn't want to leave this moment just yet. Her anger, worries and fears washed away in front of her down the current. It was so peaceful, she could almost forget that the man beside her had upended her life. She could almost forget that she despised him for working with Brian to manipulate her brother. Indeed, she was dangerously close to enjoying Cormac's company, lingering in this bubble of calm that followed the warrior everywhere he went.

"What challenges did you have to pass in order to become one of the Fianna?"

She'd heard from her brother and her mother that the men in Brian's Fianna were of exceptional skill and strength, and they'd had to prove so to join the band of warriors. Niamh had mentioned something about studying poetry and music. But she'd never heard what specific tasks they'd been given to do.

"Our first task was to memorize and then perform the twelve books of poetry of the people of Éire. Then, with only a staff and a shield, we had to defend ourselves from the spears of nine men while we stood in a hole to our waist."

Astrid nodded. "Difficult, but doable. What else?" she prompted, her curiosity piqued.

"We had to outrun a pursuer through thick foliage without being injured or breaking any branches." He looked at her askance, a sparkle of mischief in his eyes. "It's harder than it sounds."

Astrid rolled her eyes. "No need to defend your masculinity. It sounds plenty hard."

A rumble of laughter escaped Cormac's lips. "There's the Astrid I know," he teased. "After the spear throwing, the most difficult challenge for many men was that of movement." He leaned forward, speaking with his hands as much as his voice. "We trained until we were able to leap over a tree of an equal height to ourselves, and then crawl beneath a branch shorter than our knees without touching it."

"That's impossible."

"Every man that came with me to Dyflin can do it," Cormac grinned, "and I wager they'd be thrilled at repeating the experience."

His grin was infectious, and Astrid returned it in spite of her best efforts. "And what other unbelievable feats have you all done?"

"We ran through the forest with all speed, until stepping on a thorn. But you must then remove it without slowing down."

Astrid rolled her eyes again at that one. "What purpose could that possibly serve?" she challenged. "Even if you could accomplish it without falling straight on your face, why is that a skill you need to prove that you have?"

"The test is of speed, but also endurance. Imagine you're being chased through the forest and you can't stop until nightfall, but you become injured. Somehow being able to attend to it without being captured could save your life and your foot."

"Fine, fine," she allowed. "It's a bit far-fetched, but I can see that one perhaps. What are the last two?"

"A test of bravery, where we must fight outnumbered but not falter or flee."

That one made sense, at least, though she found it unsettling that he'd done that already. The image of him fighting a battle outnumbered and unable to escape made her stomach drop. She'd have to ask him more about that later.

"And the last one?" she asked.

"To marry for love, of course." His voice fell softer than a spring rain. "But you knew that one already."

A flush warmth overtook her, despite the chilly evening, gone as soon as it came. "Those are all impressive feats. I find it difficult to believe that anyone could do those things, let alone enough men to create a band of warriors."

"There's a reason we number only eight. We lost a lot of men during the spear throwing and in the battle. And a good many more were discounted for their inability to perform the other tasks."

"How many did you begin with?"

"Over fifty."

They sat a few minutes in silence once more. Astrid still didn't want to leave just yet, but the cold threatened to overpower her desire to remain out by the river with Cormac. She shivered, rubbing her arms with her hands and trying to warm herself so they could sit a bit longer in peace. It felt different when she was alone with him, comforting and exciting all at once.

"Odin's bollocks!" she swore when a violent shiver set her teeth to chattering.

Cormac chuckled at her outburst. He turned to her, his thoughtful eyes assessing as a softness overcame his face.

Astrid felt herself pulled toward him as though by a string.

His hand lifted, reaching for her.

Butterflies shot through her stomach. Was he going to pull her into his arms to warm her?

Did she want him to?

Their eyes met, and Astrid's breath caught as his hand neared her. Had he gone mad?

But he changed course before he reached her, his hand shifting from her waist to float in front of her as an offering. "We should get you to a warm fire."

Disappointment flooded Astrid. An odd thing, since it wasn't like she wanted him to touch her. She took his hand, allowing him to help her up from the soggy ground, and they began the long uphill climb to Sitric's hall.

"Tell me of Odin."

She couldn't have heard that correctly. "What?"

"I hear his name often enough, but I know very little about him."

Astrid's eyes blinked several times, as though she could clear her surprise away. "I've always liked the tale of the creation of humankind."

It seemed like a good place to start, if he truly wished to learn stories of the gods.

"Odin, Vili, and Vé were three brothers, just as you and your brothers—" She paused, remembering that Cormac actually had a fourth brother, though she hadn't realized it until just a few hours ago. She continued, deciding to stay clear of discussions of his family. "They walked together along the ocean's seething shore." She tried her best to recall the verbiage used by the skalds. "They are Aesir, powerful creators and rulers of men."

"They are gods," he interrupted.

"Yes, shush. As they walk, they spy two pieces of driftwood so big that the brothers must work together to move them further ashore. As they move the driftwood, they feel the potential of each piece deep in their bones. The wood is alive, or it could be."

Cormac walked beside her in silence, but instead of looking ahead, he glanced at her constantly, as captivated by the story now as she had been as a child.

"Using their hands, they tear into the wood, carving it, shaping it, with no tools at all. When they finish, two new creatures like there have never before been on the earth stand lifeless before them: a man and a woman.

"But they are not finished. Odin shares his breath with them, bringing them to life, but they are still figures of wood, covered in bark like the trees they came from. So Vé steps forward. He touches their eyes, ears, and mouths, granting them sight, hearing, and the ability to speak.

"Finally, Vili approaches. He places his hands on their heads and awakens their minds. He grants them movement as well and, when he finishes, the man and the woman can finally break free of their wooden casings. They move about, talking with one another and exploring the world before them.

"Seeing the creatures they have made, the gods decide they need names. Askr, the ash tree, the father of all men. Embla, the elm tree, the mother of all women. And that is one reason why Odin is the All-Father, for he and his brothers created all of us."

"I like that story," Cormac whispered, his breath turning to steam in the darkening night. "You should tell me more the next time we speak."

Astrid nibbled her lower lip, uncertain what to say next and uncertain why she was having such a reaction to this man. Only a fortnight ago, she couldn't stand him.

She still couldn't stand him. But even as the thought crossed her mind, an emotion alarmingly similar to disappointment fell over her as she watched Cormac walk away from her and into the hall. Astrid would need to take great care going forward in her interactions with Cormac. Because caring for him could only cause problems for them both.

CHAPTER FOURTEEN

ORMAC, LEFT SUDDENLY to his own devices, entered the hall to find it uncomfortably full. All he wanted to do was turn straight around and sneak into his room, avoiding all of the chaos before him. He didn't have any problem spending leisure time with his friends. Even an evening spent gaming with Sitric and his men was fun enough, but he much preferred quiet evenings with a few friends to the chaos of the hall. At least with so many people stuffing the building, Cormac had a good chance of avoiding his father and brother. He needed time to recharge before he took on that particular challenge.

Winding through the thick press of bodies, Cormac squeezed his way back to his brothers, who already sat at the table they shared with Sitric and his family. Sitric wasn't sitting now. He plied the crowd with smiles and hugs.

"There you are," Conan greeted him, handing him a flagon of ale.

Cormac fell into a seat to the left of his brother, taking the offering gratefully.

"We wondered where you'd gone off to." Diarmid leaned forward so he could see past Conan as he spoke to Cormac.

"Didn't all the other competitors go to bathe?" Cormac asked.

Conan nodded. "Most, but you must have gone off somewhere different."

Cormac shrugged, deciding it best not to comment on his time alone with Astrid. He wasn't certain how he felt about it, and he certainly wasn't prepared to discuss it with anyone else.

"Have you spoken with father at all? We haven't been over to see him or Teague yet." Diarmid looked around the room. "Though I don't know that I'd even be able to find them in this mess."

"So many people that even my boisterous brother finds it overwhelming," Cormac mused aloud. "You should tell Sitric of his grand accomplishment."

"I think they're here for an alliance with Sitric against Brian," Conan said, returning to Diarmid's question. "I'm not even certain it matters whether Teague wins or not."

"I think it does," Diarmid argued. "If Sitric formed an alliance with Father behind Brian's back, but publicly at the tournament, Brian would get word of it and likely retaliate."

"And, let's not forget that Cahill fought against Sitric in the battle that lost him Dyflin last winter," Cormac added. "A marriage might smooth out any ill will that remained from the battle."

Both his brothers nodded in agreement, all three of them taking long drinks of their tart, smoky ale.

"So you think that if Teague doesn't win, there won't be an alliance." Diarmid summarized.

Conan grinned at him. "Then I suppose you'll have to make certain Teague doesn't win."

"He won't," Cormac vowed, though uncertainty threaded his thoughts. He took another swig of his ale, his best attempt to wash down the discomfort of this entire situation.

Across the table, luminous scarlet tresses caught the firelight, glittering like a beacon from within a cloud of hungry suitors. The men swarmed Astrid like flies, buzzing around and vying for her attention.

Every nerve in his body frayed at the sight of Astrid drowning in so many men. His teeth ground and he took another drink, trying yet again to force himself to a state of calm.

It wasn't as though he had any real claim to her. Indeed, it wasn't even as though he meant to actually marry her. His entire purpose in this arrangement was to get her out of a marriage. Why, then, did he feel the need to stride over and yank them away from her? It was all he could do to keep himself from tossing each and every one of them into the mud outside the hall and onto their pandering arses.

While the guests devoured the meal, Cormac found a brief reprieve from the torture of watching Astrid defend herself from across the large table. Conversation waned while everyone filled their bellies with the warm, delicious meal of roast salmon and root vegetables.

Before the last plates had even been cleared, however, the room returned to the lawless battlefield that it had been when Cormac first entered. Lively music beckoned from the far end of the hall for those brave enough to ford their way to the dance floor. The men reappeared, once more surrounding Astrid, and this time their gesturing indicated that they were doing their best to win a dance with her.

It didn't matter. He could always interfere if needed, but if he went over there now, he would look just as foolish as the rest of them.

"You seem distracted tonight, brother."

Cormac turned to find Diarmid gone, no doubt off with his betrothed, Cara. Conan grinned at him, nodding gently toward Astrid.

"I wouldn't want to be surrounded by so many fools," Cormac grumbled, "and I doubt she does either."

"If it's bothering you so much, maybe you should go do something about it."

Cormac considered it. Indeed, the idea weighed heavily on his mind for much of the meal, until he reached an unsettling conclusion.

He may actually care for Astrid.

But Cormac held no illusions that the princess would ever return the sentiment. If he made it too obvious that he had an actual interest in her, she might end their bargain, and perhaps even choose Teague or Cairell as her new champion. Cormac doubted that any of the other warriors would agree to the deal she'd offered, particularly since she had far less leverage on them than she had on Cormac, yet the thought rattled him.

She'd only chosen him because she thought that he disliked her and wouldn't actually want to marry her. Well that, and because of his part in pushing her brother to see her wed. If she discovered that, in spite of his best efforts, he was growing fond of her, things would go back to the way they'd been—Cormac convincing Sitric to marry Sláine while Astrid did everything in her power to dissuade him. Cormac hoped she wouldn't turn on him so quickly, but he wasn't willing to risk it.

As much as he wished to retire to the solitude of his quarters, he wasn't about to abandon Astrid in a sea of drunken suitors, though he was impressed with how well she handled the onslaught. He settled in beside Conan, prepared to stay in the hall until their advances died down for the night.

In the midst of his struggle to ignore the absurd display of the men accosting Astrid, Conan smacked him on the shoulder. He nodded his head once again, as he always did to subtly sign, but this time he indicated toward one of the suitors who had peeled away from Astrid.

Their brother Teague prowled straight toward them, his deep brown eyes fixed on Cormac.

CHAPTER FIFTEEN

T HEY WERE EVERYWHERE.

Reaching, talking, asking. Occasionally shouting. They lurked like crows on a battlefield.

Luckily, Astrid thrived in chaos, though she couldn't remember a time when she'd had so many people speaking to her at once. She couldn't understand what most of them said as they spoke over one another, but that was just fine. Perhaps Sitric had been onto something when he suggested that she meet them individually, for there was no possibility of her making sense of the conversations surrounding her while they all happened concurrently.

She'd have been far more annoyed, if not for the surreptitious glances she stole toward Cormac. It entertained her to no end, watching the progression of his obvious jealousy.

First, his eyes bored murderously into each and every man at her side, as though he could hurl them away from across the vast table. Then, she'd noted the white knuckles on his hand as he gripped his ale flagon tighter and tighter. That one had been particularly entertaining. Finally, when she'd grown bold enough to meet his gaze, she saw that he clenched his teeth so tightly he probably had broken a tooth.

At the same time as it amused her, it also brought back to life that warm, tingly feeling—the one that had started deep in her belly, growing stronger the longer she kept Cormac company on the riverbank. It irritated her far more than any of the suitors. Her reactions to Cormac were getting out of control, and that simply could not stand.

But it was fine, she assured herself numerous times over the course of the meal. Just because her body seemed to like something about the warrior didn't mean she actually *cared* for him, or anything equally ridiculous. They were simply working together to accomplish goals. That was it.

And that was all it could be.

Long before the skalds took up their instruments, filling the room with lively music, and long after the dancing began, Astrid's attention split equally between the suitors surrounding her and the brooding man across the table from her. As much as she tried to ignore him, her gaze kept landing where he and his brother sat in conversation.

One of the suitors to her left—a tall, thin man who, in spite of his height over her, did not even come close to Cormac's great stature—extended his hand, requesting a dance. Astrid turned to him so that she could decide whether or not she would accept, catching movement in the corner of her eye.

Teague peeled himself away from the group of men surrounding her. It didn't take Astrid long to understand his intent. Though he wove his way around through the thick crowd, it was clear he drifted toward his brothers.

All other distractions melted away as she watched him approach Cormac and Conan. She couldn't see Teague's face until he took a position behind the two warriors, leaning down and speaking to them. She couldn't tell what was said, except that it was malicious, based on the sneer that crossed Teague's lips and the fury that filled Conan's face.

True to his patient nature, Cormac sat still, unflinching against the verbal assault. Teague's narrowed eyes and the quick movements of his pursed lips told her exactly the nature of what he said, even without her hearing any of the words. Astrid had witnessed enough men posturing over one or another to know it when she saw it.

Up until that point in the evening, Astrid had been mildly irritated. Constant interruptions were one thing, but watching someone accosting Cormac elicited quite a different reaction in her.

The blood in her veins boiled.

She knew Cormac would say nothing. He would simply sit and take whatever drivel Teague spewed at him. That was how he always reacted or, rather, didn't react, when she gave him a piece of her own mind. Cormac's nose flared, his gaze hardening as his brother leaned further down to whisper directly into his ear.

That was the moment Astrid snapped. Enough was enough. Cormac may be just fine sitting there taking it, but Astrid couldn't watch this happen. She stood, turning to the men surrounding her and clearing her throat to get their collective attention.

"I will begin meeting each of you this night to determine whether we might make a good match, should you be skilled enough to win this tournament. You will leave me be until you are summoned."

Astrid didn't wait for their reaction, instead marching around the end of the table by the same route she'd seen Teague use only moments earlier. She blew in like a storm, interrupting the conversation between the men. She stepped in between Teague and his brothers, crossing her arms and doing her best not to simply hurl insults straight at the man.

"Were you planning to actually try to win this contest?" she demanded. "Or did you come here simply to insult your own kin?"

Teague's brows rose and his eyes widened, though he didn't redden at the cheeks as Astrid often did when provoked.

"You will escort me to one of the quieter seating areas in this hall, and you will explain to me why I should even consider marrying a man who would treat his brothers in such a manner. Taunting an opponent is one thing, but seeking out and attacking your own kin is quite another. I should like to hear your justification of such behavior during a holiday celebration."

Properly chastised, Teague quietly followed Astrid, though she caught the parting glare he left with his brothers. Cormac stared at her intently as Conan fought a fit of laughter.

They moved to the quietest of the four corners of the room, where her brother had set up areas perfect for conversation or gaming, or even working on embroidery. Furs covered a circle of couches and chairs, with extra blankets piled up so that one could be comfortable to the point of laziness. Two unfamiliar women occupied the space, but left without argument when Astrid requested privacy.

"My apologies, my lady," Teague opened, taking a seat opposite her in the corner. "I swear to you it won't happen again."

His immediate apology and promise of improved behavior did a great deal to pacify Astrid's bubbling fury. "Why would you do such a thing in the first place?"

"Years ago, when the three of them were fostering with Brian, my father had a falling out with him." Teague shook his head and took a deep breath, as though fortifying himself. "It happened when he married Dunla, the night of the wedding feast. Brian and my father argued in the middle of everyone, shouting and making a show of it. After that father and I left, but Cormac and the other two stayed. We remained loyal to Malachy, the true high king. They chose to support Brian in his efforts to usurp that throne from him."

"But until the argument, your father and Brian had been friends?" Astrid hadn't heard this particular tale. All she knew was that Brian and Cahill were enemies. He was the staunchest supporter of Brian's rival Malachy.

"Aye," Teague answered. "Good enough friends that my father offered my sister to Brian when he was in need of a wife, and sent all four of us to foster with him until we came of age."

"Divided loyalties can cause great difficulty in a family," Astrid observed, "but I would ask that you keep your family feud out of this tournament."

"Of course, lady," Teague agreed. "But I'm not the one you're going to need to mind. It's my father who's bitter over it."

That bit of information didn't surprise Astrid, though she worried about the disruption it might cause in the future. If Cahill proved problematic, she or her brother or even her mother could speak with him. For the time being, she was pleased with her pacification of Teague, who had been far more civil than she expected considering how she'd approached him. Many men raised their hackles the moment a woman challenged them. She tried not to do it often but, as her brother liked to point out, keeping her thoughts to herself was one of her greater struggles.

Standing and following Teague back toward the rest of the merriment, Astrid hoped that her announcement encouraged the gaggle of suitors who'd been following her like goslings to disperse. Instead, she found every one of them standing there, staring at her expectantly.

Waiting for their turn.

Astrid sighed. This was going to be a long night.

CHAPTER SIXTEEN

THE FOLLOWING MORN, a storm broke out over Dyflin. Clouds as black as his father's soul rolled in, darkening the skies and bringing sheets of rain, forcing everyone indoors.

Early in the day, before the tournament was set to begin, the Fianna met in their guest hall to discuss the appearance of Cahill and Teague. Cormac had ground his teeth through the entire conversation, but was glad of his companions' willingness to help him and his brothers address the issue. Everyone agreed that Cahill had come to seek an alliance. They needed to know the terms of his proposal, and whether Sitric was inclined to accept them. By the end of their brief discussion, Diarmid promised to speak with Sitric and attempt to learn his feelings while dissuading him from the alliance. Cormac and Conan would speak with Teague and Cahill to discover what they could about their aims in Dyflin and do their best to deter them from allying with Sitric.

Undaunted by the prospect of a day trapped indoors, Sitric declared the beginning of the *hnefatafl* tournaments. Servants produced a collection of boards that they set up at the long feasting tables in the center of the hall. Eight boards, four to a table, afforded the men space to pair off and battle one another in wit as opposed to strength.

Though guests came to watch the matches, the hall wasn't filled to bursting while they waited out the weather. Grateful that he had room to breathe and think, Cormac had little difficulty besting his opponents. Most of the men hadn't played the game before and had to spend time learning and practicing before their skill could truly be measured. Sitric recruited Astrid, Finn, Dallan, and several of his warriors to take a man and teach him to play the game properly.

Cormac kept an eye out for opportunities to pull Astrid aside and thank her for shooing away his brother. Though he was more than capable of enduring Teague's harassment, he understood that she went out of her way to help him. She'd come from nowhere as his self-appointed champion, something he found entirely too endearing. She cleaved into his brother as a spear cuts through a boar's gut, rendering him speechless and shockingly compliant. Cormac would not soon forget the look on Teague's face, and for that alone she'd earned his gratitude.

The hearthfire crackled merrily while the games got underway. The occasional outburst of laughter or frustration interrupted the blessed quiet, but overall the morning passed in peace. Between his own matches and Astrid's time spent instructing, Cormac didn't find a moment to pull her aside and thank her properly until after the midday meal.

It was a small affair, with just enough of last night's leftovers to tide everyone over until dinner in the late afternoon. The men, including Sitric, grew weary of the endless games of *hnefatafl*, and the rain no longer pattered against the rooftop.

"We will cease our contests for the next few hours," Sitric announced. "Enjoy the fine day and we will see you for dinner. But be aware that I may, at my pleasure, announce a contest of strength following supper." He grinned like a madman. "Or not."

Following Sitric's devious announcement, a slow trickle of folk wandered out the front doors of the feasting hall, which told Cormac that the weather must have cleared. Astrid joined those leaving the hall, spurring Cormac into action.

"My lady," he called, getting her attention.

She turned to him, her smile so bright it halted his next step. Cormac felt a tightness in his chest, a desire to pull her into his arms. He fought that instinct like a foe on the battlefield. She wasn't smiling at him, anyway. She never smiled at him. He'd simply caught her in an unguarded moment.

"Where is everyone going?" he asked when he reached her.

"We're collecting evergreen branches to decorate the hall for the *Jól* season," she explained.

"How much would it bother you if I came along?"

The smile slipped from her face, replaced with a flicker of fire in those honey gold eyes. "The usual amount."

"Excellent." She hadn't said he *couldn't* come along. "I could use some fresh air."

With surprisingly little opposition from Astrid, he followed her out into the chilly winter afternoon. They strolled at a pleasant pace down the hill from Sitric's hall and into the town proper of Dyflin. It was a track that Cormac had travelled many times over the course of his stay there, as it was the only road that led from Sitric's holding into the village. To get anywhere outside the king's halls, Cormac used this path. The air held a crispness that made Cormac glad of his fur-lined cloak.

He glanced at Astrid to ensure that she wore enough clothing to keep her warm. This time a cloak of deepest green, the same shade as the pine trees they approached outside of town, draped her delicate shoulders. The white and black ermine lining would keep her warm enough.

They reached a copse of trees—pine, fir, and juniper—and the villagers began grabbing branches that had fallen. Cormac did the same, picking up a sap-covered fir branch, long and thin and still holding onto some of its cones.

"I wanted to thank you," he told Astrid as she walked beside him through the small but thick forest of evergreens. "It was kind of you to distract Teague, that Conan and I might continue in peace."

"It was nothing," she brushed off, picking up a wild-looking branch. "I needed to speak with him anyway, and I meant what I told him. I have no interest whatsoever in a man who can't be respectful to his own kin."

Cormac smiled at that, continuing to pick up branches as they walked. "Either way, you were a fearsome sight to behold. He'll think twice about crossing you in the future. And it was rather enjoyable to not be the one under attack for a change."

She looked up at him, her eyes sparkling topazes. "Don't tell me that Cormac, the great warrior of the Gaels, can't take one Ostman princess."

"Believe me, princess—I could take you." The words were out before he'd fully comprehended their implication. Not that his lack of thought made them any less true. But, had he taken a moment, he'd not have let them escape.

Astrid's eyes went wide, her pink lips parting at his statement.

He'd rendered her speechless, he realized as she continued to stare at him. "Don't tell me that the mouthy Ostman princess has finally been bested by one measly Gaelic warrior," he prodded, relishing her reaction more than he ought.

"Don't be ridiculous," she snapped, breathing in deeply and shifting the armful of branches she carried.

The skies opened again before Cormac could poke her further. Instead of angry torrents that raged across the landscape, it floated in a soft mist, that, combined with the chilly air, turned into the first snow he'd seen in a long while. It didn't snow often on the island, and it happened even less that the snow stuck for any length of time. Giggles and gasps filled the small forest, where everyone enjoyed the rare gift of snow in the *Jól* season as they foraged.

Cormac turned to Astrid, the smile on her face pinching his chest. It was a smile he liked more every time he saw it, though it still wasn't for him. She gazed up in wonder at the snowflakes falling above her head. They landed across her shoulders, her freckled cheeks, and dusted her red hair in a thin layer of white. She looked every inch the Ostman princess that she was, a princess of winter snows and stormy seas. Or a princess of elm, according to her story, with a woodland green cloak to match the forest surrounding them.

A trio of children tore through the trees beside them, laughing and giggling, chasing snowflakes with their mouths open and their tongues out. They laughed so much, Cormac doubted that they caught any, but they seemed to be having a fine time anyway.

"I've always wanted children," Astrid said quietly after the little ones left the glade.

Her candidness intrigued Cormac. "Then why fight a marriage so fiercely?"

Astrid sighed, turning toward him. "Because the only marriage my brother seeks is one to a Gael," she replied. "My children will be raised as Ostmen—speaking our language, following our traditions." She worried her bottom lip, just as she had the night she bargained with him, afraid for her future.

"I think you're afraid," Cormac challenged.

Astrid narrowed her eyes at him. "Well, I suppose that's what I get for trying to be civil."

Cormac took a step nearer, advancing. "And now you're avoiding the topic." He felt like a wolf on the hunt, finally nearing his prey. He'd almost gotten her to have a real conversation with him, and he wasn't going to give up the chase just yet.

"What is it you want me to say, exactly?" she challenged, ever ready for battle.

He was close enough now that he could smell more than just the pine trees. A delicate, sweet fragrance filled the air between them—it could only be Astrid. Something primal and long forgotten came to life, drawing him even closer to her.

"We fear only that which we cannot control," he whispered. "You can ensure that your children learn all those things, no matter your husband. I want you to tell me what you are really afraid of."

He didn't think she would really do it. When her shoulders fell in defeat and the light left her eyes, he knew he'd struck true.

"If I lose my brother, my mother, the people here in Dyflin, and the traditions we share..." She went quiet for a long while.

"I'm afraid I would lose myself, too."

Her answer was so honest, so raw, and so unexpected that it tore at Cormac's heart. He closed the small distance left between them.

Without thinking, he raised his hand to gently cup her porcelain face. Flecks of snow tickled his palm, icy pinpricks against his fingers. "The man matters more than the culture." His fingers caressed the smooth skin of her cheek. "A good man will help you hold onto the things that matter. Whether Gael or Ostman or something else entirely."

Her honey-colored gaze clouded over with desire. He couldn't look away. He couldn't stop touching her. His thumb brushed her bottom lip, and he realized that if he did nothing to stop himself, he would kiss her.

More alarmingly, he realized that he wanted to do just that.

Astrid's lips parted invitingly, her breath a puff of white between them.

His heart raced, his body ached. He couldn't risk it. Before he made a bigger mess of the situation, he dropped his hand back to his side and stepped away, heading for the hall.

How could he have let that happen? Where had his years of training and discipline gone?

He'd come so close to kissing her, to giving her a real reason to reject him and ruining his only chance of convincing Sitric to wed Sláine. Even still, his fingers ached at the memory of her soft skin beneath his hands. As he climbed the hill to Sitric's hall, he berated himself. He had utterly failed at the one thing he wanted to accomplish.

Because after that appalling lack of self-control, Astrid would have no doubts about his growing feelings toward her.

CHAPTER SEVENTEEN

T HE SUN ROSE hot the following morning, providing enough warmth to offset the chill that gripped the air these days. Astrid pulled her cloak tighter about her shoulders as she strode across the tournament field toward the temporary halls they'd constructed for their competitors. The breakfasting hour had not yet come to an end, and Astrid hoped to catch Cairell at his morning meal so she could finish these cursed interviews.

He was the only one she hadn't managed to meet with two nights prior. She knew that she'd been putting off this particular conversation, though she couldn't imagine why. As her brother had pointed out that first day, Cairell may be her best chance at a marriage to a fellow Ostman. Perhaps, instead of avoiding it, Astrid should take this interview more seriously.

And, perhaps, that was precisely why she'd been avoiding it.

She shouldn't want Cormac. She *couldn't* want Cormac. And yet, all she'd thought about since they stood together in the snow yesterday was the feel of his hand on her cheek, warm against the bite of the winter air, and the look in his eyes as he stared into hers. Gods, she'd have sworn he was about to kiss her.

Even worse, her treacherous body had *wanted* him to kiss her. Shoving that appalling revelation into the back of her mind, she opened the doors to the hall where Cairell quartered.

These halls, as they were temporary, didn't have large central hearths like the ones in their holding. Instead braziers lined the narrow corridors around the edge of the hall's center, casting a soft orange glow on the room. Compared with the chaos of the past few days, the halls on the gaming field felt oddly quiet, empty enough that the servants' footfalls echoed hollowly between the timbered walls.

A few folk sat at the tables finishing up their morning meals. Astrid had skipped her own, with little appetite this particular morn. All she wanted was to get this interview out of the way, and to get Cormac out of her mind.

Just as she'd hoped, she found Cairell sitting at one of the tables breaking his fast.

"May I join you?" she asked, walking over and standing opposite him.

He grinned up at her, his thick, golden brown beard wiggling as he did so. "I wondered when I'd get my chance with you," he replied, gesturing that she should indeed take the seat across from him.

"I'm sorry that I wasn't able to meet with you the other night," she began. "It had simply grown too late, and I'm afraid I wouldn't have been a very good conversationalist." Astrid did not mention that she could have very well found him yesterday, but instead had gone on a walk with Cormac and nearly kissed him. The very thought of his name brought a tightness to her core, a sensation that had become irritatingly frequent these days.

"Did you see the snow yesterday?" Cairell asked.

"I did," Astrid replied with a small smile. She should be the one leading this conversation, yet her thoughts continued to return to Cormac, to the way he looked at her. His eyes fiercely blue, their intent perfectly clear.

She needed to get him out of her mind.

And Cairell may be her best chance of doing just that.

"It was a lovely surprise for this time of year," she added, realizing her answer had been insufficient.

"So what manner of questions have you been asking the men? I admit, I've been curious as to what these discussions might entail."

"It depends on the man," Astrid told him. "Often I ask of their family and how their life is, where they came from, the arrangement of their keep or their town."

Astrid also made a point of including a question or two to gauge how they might treat a wife. She found that their thoughts on female relatives were often quite telling, but she liked to prod them more deliberately to see what sort of reaction it got her. The last thing Astrid wanted, aside from leaving her home and going somewhere far from her own people, was to marry a man who might mistreat her.

"And what manner of questions do you have for me, then," he prompted, taking a bite of bacon.

Astrid already determined that Cairell was not a man with violent tendencies toward women. Sometimes she spoke with a man and could tell instantly that he could be cruel when his temper was prodded. But the man before her showed a great deal of patience, for Astrid knew that her mind was far afield and she'd not been a good conversation partner thus far.

"My questions for you are different from those I've asked any other of the men," she replied.

"It's because of my mother, isn't it?" he asked. "She came with me, excited at the prospect of spending time in a settlement of her own people."

His words were answer enough for one of Astrid's questions. Apparently his home was not a settlement of her people, as she'd hoped, or anything close to it.

"Should I assume from that statement that there are no other Ostmen in your homeland?"

He shook his head, the grin slipping from his face. "I wish I could tell you otherwise, but it's only my mother and a few others."

"My grandmother was an Ostman servant to a Gaelic king," she told him.

"I had heard that, lady, and I thought it an interesting connection between us."

It was, indeed, and Astrid already found him far more promising than any of the other men, aside from her chosen champion.

"Do any of them speak *Norróna*?" she asked, hoping that perhaps, even if there was a dearth of representation, she may at least have fellow Ostmen with whom to share the language. That would make it far easier to raise her children speaking it as she wished to do.

Cairell grinned, this time setting down his breakfast and giving her his undivided attention. "Aye, all the Ostmen do," he replied in the language.

Astrid straightened in surprise. Perhaps there was some hope of preserving her culture after all. Her mission completed and all her questions answered, Astrid took her leave, wishing him well in the games to come. She had heard quite enough by that point to make her assessment.

He was a fairly pleasant fellow, similar to her brother in disposition with his proclivity for grinning and the odd wry comment. Unfortunately, the answers to her most pressing questions left something to be desired. Cairell may share a heritage and a language with her, but it sounded like living in his kingdom would be nothing like living in Dyflin. It still wouldn't feel like home, and Astrid still ran the very real risk of a cool reception there with so few of her own people.

Her decision firmly in hand, Astrid returned to her family's hall to find an alarming surprise awaiting her. Her brother, bent head-to-head over a *hnefatafl* board.

With Princess Catrin.

"How goes your game?" Astrid called, striding over to interrupt with all haste.

"She's doing well." Sitric sat back from the table, smiling up at Astrid. Her brother always smiled.

"It's more difficult than I expected, given how small the board," Catrin giggled.

"Thank you for playing with me." He stood, straightening his red tunic and turning to Astrid. "I'm glad you're here. I need to speak with you and mother."

"Of course," Astrid replied, happy to have succeeded with her interruption. "I'll go fetch her."

"No need," Gormla called, rising from a couch in the far corner of the hall. "She's already here."

Catrin, somehow, didn't sense that she was being dismissed.

"Could you give us a moment, dear?" Sitric asked her.

"Oh! Of course." She bobbed a sloppy curtsy before scurrying from the hall.

Gormla joined Astrid and Sitric at the table, inspecting the game of *hnefatafl* underway and taking Catrin's next move for her. "I'm not sure this can be salvaged," she muttered, shaking her head.

"I assure you, it can't," Sitric laughed. "But she had fun, and she's only just learning."

"You need a cleverer wife than that," Astrid told him.

"I've bigger problems than a wife, at present." He paced instead of sitting, a sure sign something troubled him in spite of his good temper. "Cahill has asked for an alliance against Brian, regardless of the outcome of the tournament. What say you?"

Gormla rapped her fingers over the oaken tabletop.

Astrid couldn't quite decide how she felt. On the one hand, a rebellion against Brian to reclaim their autonomy was exactly what she wanted. But on the other, Cahill had only recently helped Brian crush them in battle. "How much do you trust him?"

Sitric's smile fell to a grimace. "Not even a little. Aside from his oath to Malachy, the man's allegiance changes with the wind."

"What did he offer, exactly?" Gormla asked.

"Men. Aid in battle. And a fair deal on trade goods."

"And how do we know for whom his men fight?" Astrid pressed. "For all we know this could be some ploy between him and Malachy to force us under their boots instead of Brian's."

"I agree with Astrid," Gormla declared. "He cannot be trusted."

"And," Astrid continued, the reasons piling up against Cahill, "does he have enough men for us to attack soon? If not, and if Brian discovers your secret dealings, the chance may never come. Brian won't take such an alliance lightly should he discover it."

Sitric stroked his long beard, still pacing. "This is why I come to you both. Ever the fonts of wisdom and insight. I shall decline his offer. And Astrid," he looked to her pointedly, "don't feel the need to grow close to Teague solely for politics."

She nodded, swallowing. There was little danger of that after the events of the opening feast. Though he wasn't a wicked man, he remained strongly in opposition to Cormac.

And, for better or for worse, Cormac was always on her mind.

CHAPTER EIGHTEEN

THUS FAR, CORMAC had managed to avoid his father and brother, aside from Teague's antagonism at the opening feast, anyway. Unfortunately, he and his brothers were tasked with determining what their father and Teague were plotting by showing up to the tournament uninvited—which meant he'd need to speak with them both, and soon.

Astrid had relayed to him the conversation she had with Teague at the feast, including a comment he made about Cahill being the one to watch. Cormac didn't like that one bit, as it implied that there was something to watch *for*. His father wouldn't be easy to taunt into speaking, but since Teague had openly made such a statement, Cormac hoped he might divulge even more with the correct motivation.

That morn, Sitric announced that the men would play games of *toga honk*, which Finn told him was a tug-of-war. Like all the other challenges, the men were matched by their respective strengths, which meant that Cormac would battle Cairell for certain, and likely his brother Teague as well.

After breaking his fast, Cormac ventured down to the guest housing outside Dyflin, near the field where they competed each day. Though Diarmid and Conan were also responsible for speaking with Teague, Cormac thought it may feel less like a conversation and more like an attack if they all descended at once. He guessed the best chance at getting some honest answers from his elder brother lay in speaking with him alone.

Cormac only needed to follow the sound of clashing steel to find Teague. A group of men sparred in the fields outside the guest halls, his brother among them. Teague wasn't in a match, so Cormac approached him and stood beside him in silence, watching the sparring currently underway.

"I'm surprised you aren't already wed," Cormac mused aloud. "As I recall, you had droves of girls following you around."

"I almost married," Teague replied, his attention still fixed on the men crossing swords. "I'm surprised Diarmid was the first to choose a wife."

"If you'd known him as a young man, you'd be even more shocked."

"Is she a good woman, his betrothed?"

"Aye. One of the best." Cormac smiled to himself. "Why did you not marry? You said you almost did."

Teague's jaw clenched, but he still didn't turn to face his brother. "The marriage wasn't deemed suitable."

"I'm sorry." Cormac meant it, too. He knew how it felt to care strongly about something only to face their father's opposition for it.

"Do you know the princess well?" Teague asked. "I've heard she can be a handful."

"You've heard right," Cormac chuckled. He didn't care at all for the idea of Astrid marrying his brother, but he held his tongue—he'd finally gotten Teague to speak civilly with him. Instead, he tried to turn the conversation toward their purpose in Dyflin. "Are you truly interested in marrying her?"

Teague shrugged. "She's not hideous, and everyone knows it's a good alliance to make."

Astrid was so far from hideous that Cormac struggled to keep his mouth shut at Teague's understatement. Instead, he decided to keep pushing. "How did you learn of the tournament?"

"I'm not going to betray him," Teague replied evenly.

An interesting response. And, again, unsettling as it implied some amount of plotting.

"It's a long way to come, from Connachta, especially if you were not invited." It had crossed Cormac's mind that perhaps they *had* been invited by Sitric, but that the invitation had been kept secret so he didn't appear a traitor to Brian. The more he reflected on it, however, the more Cormac thought that Sitric likely held as much of a grudge against Cahill as he did against Brian, since both kings attacked Dyflin.

Dyflin brought Cahill within easy reach of Brian's fortresses, but without an army it wouldn't do much good.

Teague scowled, turning to Cormac. "What do you want?"

"To make sure you didn't come here to do more than just win a bride."

"*I* came here solely for the tournament."

Cormac didn't like the way Teague emphasized that statement. "And father?"

"As I said," his voice turned to thunder, "unlike you, I won't betray him."

THE GAMES THEMSELVES proved little challenge for Cormac after the rigorous trials he'd undergone to join the Fianna, which meant that his most pressing problems at present remained his father's plotting and his relationship with Astrid.

Was she angry with him? Did she plan to end their agreement after he stepped so egregiously out of line? Or, perhaps the most frightening possibility of all, did she return his feelings? For after that moment with her in the trees, Cormac had no choice but to accept that his affections toward her grew by the day in spite of his efforts to quash them.

At midday, Cormac stood shoulder to shoulder with his brothers, surrounded by the rest of the Fianna, waiting to be called for his turn at the *toga honk*. The contest began with the weakest men paired off, and would work up to the strongest. Cormac remained with the Fianna to watch the first bouts and gain insight into strategies he might use to overpower his opponent.

From what he observed, it seemed the most advantageous to keep your legs at a wide stance and use them to anchor you while gripping the rope somewhere near your waist. The men who braced their legs one in front and one behind tended to be the ones that lost. He also noted that men struggled when they held the rope too high or too low from their waists. Once he felt confident in his strategy, Cormac made his way through the crowd of onlookers until he reached Astrid.

After careful consideration, he determined that the best course of action was to continue helping her find a solution to the problem of an unwanted marriage. He'd come up with another idea, though every time he thought of it he liked it less. But still, it was the best he had to offer and, in the end, it was Astrid's decision—not his.

She spotted him before he came within earshot, and instead of forcing him to fetch her, she excused herself from her brother and mother and met him toward the back of the crowd.

"Is something the matter?" she asked, her brows knitted.

Cormac took a deep breath. He didn't want to ask, but he needed an answer. "Do you want me to let him win?"

Astrid's brows only furrowed further, her eyes narrowing. "What?"

"I thought," he hesitated, choosing his words with care. "He's the closest you'll find to the husband that you wanted. If you desire it, I will allow him to win so that you can have your Ostman husband."

Astrid's mouth fell open. Clearly, he'd taken her by surprise. That she hadn't even been considering such a thing gave him some small hope. Her mouth opened and closed several times, as though slowly collecting her answer with each motion before she could finally get it out.

Before she managed an answer, Cormac was called to the field for his turn.

"Good luck." Her whispered words followed him all the way to the rope.

It was, in keeping with Astrid's manner, the least helpful answer to his question.

Cairell picked up the far end of the thick rope. Cormac went to the near end and did the same. The rope was heavy, as thick as the palm of his hands, which made it more difficult to grip. It reminded Cormac of a ship's rope, as though Sitric had taken a spare from the harbor. The ends of it were rough and fraying from the friction of the other men's grips. Between Cormac and Cairell, beneath the center of the rope, a bed of red hot coals crackled. The first man to place his feet in the coals lost.

"Pull!" Sitric's man shouted once Cormac and Cairell were in position.

And pull they did.

Cormac's hands tightened about the rope, his legs standing firm as he leaned backward. He knew that he could win, but if anyone here could beat him, it was Cairell. Cormac needed to watch for an opportunity to overpower him or to outlast him. Fixing his eyes on Cairell, Cormac tugged at the rope with all his might, taking one shaky step backward.

With a guttural cry, Cairell stumbled one step closer to the crackling coals. He pulled hard on the rope, digging in his heels and throwing his back into the movement.

Cormac's muscles strained against the pull, but excitement rushed through him in spite of the discomfort. Cairell had faltered in his form sooner than Cormac expected. Once more, Cormac tugged the rope forcefully. This time, he put all his weight into jogging backwards.

Cairell flew forward, his feet flying across the hot coals and his oath echoing across the field.

Cheering broke across the crowd like a crashing wave.

He'd done it. For better or for worse, Cormac had bested Cairell. Dropping the rope, he hurried to help the poor man out of the bed of coals. Then he headed straight for Finn, though the rest of the Fianna waylaid him en route, congratulating him just as heartily as they always did.

"Well done." Finn grabbed his elbow, pulling him into a hug.

"Thank you." Cormac leaned nearer. "I have a favor to ask."

"Anything," Finn told him.

Cormac wetted his lips, looking around at the crowd and lowering his voice. "I'd like you to teach me the Ostman tongue."

Finn's eyes went wide, a smile overtaking his face. "Any particular reason?

Cormac shook his head. He could barely admit the reason to himself. He'd certainly not speak with anyone else about it, not even his closest friends. Not yet. Eventually, though, he'd have to tell them the decision he'd reached. He didn't just want to win the tournament.

He wanted to win Astrid's heart as well.

CHAPTER NINETEEN

WHAT IN THE world was wrong with her?

Astrid stood watching the Fianna congratulate Cormac, still in shock over the short interaction they'd just had. He gave her an escape. He'd presented her with a solution.

And instead of doing the intelligent thing and taking it, she'd frozen up.

More and more each day, her uncertainty about what she really wanted deepened, and every time she spoke with Cormac, her resolve crumbled a little further. The pain in his voice when he'd asked if she wanted to wed Cairell had struck her like a blow. It hurt her to imagine that he thought she might desire someone else, but it confused her just as much to admit the reason why.

The crowd roared as Garvan, one of the smaller men who'd just defeated his second opponent, raised his arms in victory. The other man, Mochta, backed quickly off of the smoking coals.

Between the din of the crowd and the commotion of the next two contestants approaching the field to take their turns at *hoga tonk*, Astrid made use of the chaos around her to broach a rather sensitive topic with her brother. Normally, she'd not dare such a conversation in public view, but she knew that no one would be able to hear them over the noise.

"You seemed to be enjoying Catrin's company yesterday."

"I thought it prudent to give both women a fair chance," he replied. "She's quite a lot of fun."

"She's quite young," Astrid countered. "Sláine is the best

choice, and I don't really see a reason to prolong it any further.

Sitric's crystal blue gaze turned toward her, piercing her to the spot. "Do I sense a sudden change in your opinion, dear sister?"

"It's not sudden at all, *dear brother*," she shot back. "Mother and I have spent time with both of the brides since last we spoke. And, as you appear determined to uphold your peace with Brian for the time being, you must choose one. *And,* if you're going to choose a bride, she may as well be a woman capable of actually helping around here. That woman is Sláine. All politics aside," she pressed, "she's the better choice."

Sitric considered her for a long moment, as though searching for a motive. "I'll have her accompany me formally to the *flyting.*"

"The *flyting?*" That was the first Astrid had heard of that particular contest.

"I thought that would be a fun one to spring on them without any training," her brother laughed. "It'll be more entertaining if they haven't prepared, and I'm interested to see what sorts of things they can come up with."

"How will they even know what to do?" Astrid groaned.

"I will explain the rules and show them a few rounds as an example. The more they drink, the more their tongues will loosen. It should prove entertaining, indeed."

"I see." Astrid narrowed her eyes. "And when do you intend to spring this on the men?"

"After we dine, sometime in the next few nights. Probably not this night or the next, though. They'll be exhausted after today, and tomorrow they revisit *knattleikr*, so not then, either. I haven't decided, but it matters not." He smiled, clearly pleased with himself. "Come now, let's see how this one turns out." He rubbed his palms together excitedly, turning his attention back to the match.

Seeing little choice in the matter, and refusing to watch Cormac make a fool of himself, Astrid procured copious amounts of ale and snuck them into Cormac's room, just as she had that first night when they'd played *hnefatafl*. He would need coaching for the *flyting*. A man of few words, he could not be trusted to win a drunken poetry contest without some help.

This time, when he returned from the feast, he looked far less surprised to find her waiting for him.

Her heart swelled in her chest as he entered the room. In that moment, Astrid realized how much she'd been looking forward to speaking with him alone again. Something about him felt so familiar. It called to her. It grounded her. She didn't know why, but she took great comfort in his presence, and the more time she spent there, the deeper she fell into it.

"That's an awful lot of ale." He eyed the two pitchers and pair of cups taking up the entirety of his bedside table. "I've already had some with dinner."

"Sitric has just informed me that he intends to spring upon you a drinking contest."

A small smile cracked at the corner of his full lips. "And you believe I need to practice drinking?" It widened to a mischievous grin, bringing to life a flutter in her stomach.

"It's not just drinking."

He walked over to join her on the bed, sitting much closer this time than he had when she was last in his room. A spark shot through her from the place where their legs touched on the edge of the bed.

"And what else might it entail?"

"You must insult your opponent in verse," she explained.

"Like a bard?" Cormac looked skeptical.

"Aye, but there are ways to do it that will best appease my brother and the other Ostmen."

"I see."

It did not sound as though he saw at all. Astrid thought he should be quite a bit more alarmed than he appeared.

"It's much more difficult than it sounds," she insisted, as though he'd made some sort of argument.

His blue eyes smoldered at her playfully. "It sounds plenty hard."

He was throwing her own words back at her, when she'd been skeptical of his Fianna challenges. "There are ways to insult and ways to get into a duel."

"Ah. Well, I'd prefer not to kill a man at a drinking contest, so what should I not do?"

"If you call a man a coward, he's within rights to attack you and to challenge you to a duel. It's not an insult to be tossed lightly, but it is permitted. Just be aware that should he take exception, he can challenge you at your accusation. The same is true of telling a man he's a fool or accusing him of treachery."

"I can't call a man a fool, but I must insult him? That I don't understand," he poured them each a cup of ale, handing one to Astrid. "Fool does not seem so deep an insult as a coward or a traitor."

"All the same, those are the three words I would stay away from the most."

Cormac nodded his understanding, but his brows furrowed as he considered her words.

"You must be poetic," she tried again. "Use beautiful but hurtful words."

Cormac sighed, taking a long drink. "I've heard the bards do something similar, but I'm not a bard, for all my training."

"Bard or not, you'll be asked to do it. Practice will help," she raised her glass, "as will the ale."

"Fine." He took a long, loud gulp of ale. "Show me."

"'Tis lucky for me that you're competing,

It gives me someone easy for beating."

Cormac burst into laughter at her rhyme. "Clever and brutal."

"Don't make them too long, either, else you run a greater risk of talking yourself into a bad rhyme." She'd seen it many a time, especially the longer the contest went on. "Now you try."

He blew out a heavy breath, setting down his ale and knitting his brows.

"Many a man can wield a sword,

"But few, indeed, are such a disgrace to their lord."

Astrid laughed so hard her ale flew back into her cup. "That was better than I expected," she admitted, unable to stop grinning. "But you need to make it more clearly personal. You didn't name the man who was a disgrace, so the insult is weakened."

She stood, taking a few steps right in front of him as she thought up another example. "Your opponent could counter it," she explained.

"How happy for me, that *you* pointed that out,

"It saves me the trouble of watching you rout."

Once again, Cormac laughed, this time so hard he had to set down his ale so it didn't spill.

Astrid couldn't help but join him. "Gods, that was awful, wasn't it?"

"Wait, wait." He held up his hands, a look of pure mischief on his face.

"Rout or rot? They're both the same,

"When spoken by a man with your stink and name."

He barely finished the last word.

Astrid doubled over at the atrocious insult, falling onto the bed beside Cormac. "I can't decide if that was awful or brilliant," she gasped between laughs.

Cormac let himself fall backward, his head facing hers on the soft blankets. His whole face lit as he looked at her, filled with infectious mirth. Blue eyes sparkled like gemstones, or like freshly fallen snow. Laying like this, so close to him, put Astrid in mind of the day they collected the evergreen boughs.

Of the day she thought he might kiss her.

Her eyes fell to his lips, to the way they pulled tightly across his face in a grin yet somehow still looked so full. Before she could shake some sense into herself, he moved toward her, sealing her thoughts with a kiss.

His lips felt just as soft and full as they looked, tasting her tentatively. She felt the smile on his face as his hand came up to her cheeks, as his nose brushed gently alongside hers.

A rush of heat flooded her body. She should stop this. She shouldn't want this. Yet, whether the ale or the atmosphere or something else entirely, Astrid let herself have this one moment. Wrapping one hand over his shoulder, she pulled herself toward him and kissed him right back.

CHAPTER TWENTY

GOOD LORD, SHE was kissing him.

By all rights, she could've smacked him and he would've deserved it. He'd fumbled his way through drinking and rhyming until he was so deep in his cups that he'd convinced himself this was a good idea.

And, somehow, she'd agreed. Instead of fleeing, she held his shoulder like a tree in a storm, her shuddering exhale disappearing into his mouth.

Every muscle in his body tightened at the taste of her on his lips, the feel of her beneath his fingers. His thoughts were too dulled by ale to be of any help, so he let it all go. There was no more hiding how he felt or what he wanted. His tongue teased her, parting her lips and deepening the kiss.

Her body rolled against his, delicious curves pressed greedily against his hardening desire. A sinful moan escaped her, sending a shiver down his back and setting a fire in his blood.

Then she pushed him away.

Astrid was up and out of the bed before he could even manage an apology. Clearly, he'd misread her. The ale had dulled his mind more than he realized, a mistake he hoped hadn't done irreparable damage.

Cursing himself for a fool, Cormac poured himself another cup of ale.

SHE DIDN'T SPEAK to him at all the next day. Or the one after that.

Or even the one after that. They played more *knattleikr* and were taught to row the longboats, leaving Cormac as exhausted physically as he was defeated mentally. He tried to corner her to properly apologize, but she managed to avoid him at every turn. He grew so distracted between trying to fix his blunder and performing in all the various matches that he completely forgot about the *flyting*.

If he'd remembered, he could've asked Finn for help. Not only was his friend a bard of great skill, he was also the son of an Ostman who had family in Éire. That would've been a good plan.

Instead, Cormac forgot it entirely and was blindsided when Sitric announced at the end of the meal one night that the *flyting* was about to begin. Beside him, Finn and Dallan laughed at his expense, happily explaining to the other Fianna precisely what Cormac was about to attempt.

Whispers shot down the hall as word of the contest spread faster than a house fire. By the time the servants had delivered an absurd amount of ale and the competitors were paired off along the table, the hall was stuffed with witnesses to his impending humiliation. And, of course, Cormac's opponent was Cairell—the Ostman. Even if he wasn't skilled in poetry, the man would have an advantage over him in knowing what was expected.

Cormac tried to pay attention to the men who went before them, but he felt as though he were suffocating. He could compete in feats of strength and endurance. He could wrestle or duel a man from dawn to dusk. But performing without preparation in front of a crowd while Astrid glared at him from the head of the table? He'd rather let Teague take after him with the *knattleikr* stick.

His turn came far too quickly. Not daring a glance at the red-haired vixen, he threw back as big a gulp of ale as he could.

"Cairell!" Sitric called cheerily. "Insult our friend, Cormac, for us!"

This could not be happening. He took one more deep drink, then braced himself for the worst.

Cairell appeared thrilled at the opportunity, diving right into a nasty rhyme.

"What does our Cormac have in common with bogs?

"Both of them stink of farts and frogs!"

The hall erupted in laughter. It wasn't a particularly dignified insult, but it was the sort that always landed with an audience—especially after enough ale. The sound of their mirth shook the hall, drowning out Cormac's thoughts as he struggled to form a response.

"Insult his mother!" Finn hissed in his ear. "They love that, too."

"Young bard," Sitric called, eyeing Finn knowingly, "why don't you come sit up here with us to help judge the contest?"

Silence descended as everyone awaited Cormac's reply. He swallowed, then did his best to follow Finn's advice.

"I may smell like muck on an oar,

"But at least my mother's not a whore."

Another round of laughter, even from Cairell himself. But his opponent must have some practice at this game, for his response came quick and cutting.

"Your mother doesn't need to be,

"For you sow your oats so wild and free,

"And that's an accomplishment, truly, a win,

"Since your prick's no bigger than a sewing pin."

Damn. That was good.

Shouts filled the room. Cormac rubbed his hand over his neck, struggling to catch his breath. He needed to come up with something clever.

But all he could do was listen to the roar surrounding him, closing in about him. He opened his mouth, but nothing came out.

He should insult the man's appearance or his skill in battle. Anything would be better than crippling silence. Cormac tried again, yet still no words came.

Knowing when he'd been bested, he raised his cup to Cairell and took a drink. "Well played," he congratulated him. "Well played."

ASTRID SAT IN shock as Cormac conceded the match. What had she expected, though? She'd ignored him all this time instead of working with him. She'd never felt so torn in her entire life.

Or so afraid.

After that kiss, she'd been so disgusted with herself, appalled at her lack of self-control. And what was more, she hadn't even been deep in her cups then. All she wanted after that was to put as much distance between them so she wouldn't be tempted again. She needed time and space to sort out her feelings on all of it. She still needed time and space, but if she wanted Cormac to win, she'd have to start helping him again.

Was that what she wanted? Sure, he made her heart pound and her stomach flutter. He held her thoughts captive for much of the day, and she could hardly wait to steal away with him for a moment when the opportunity presented itself. But was that enough? Was a physical desire for a man reason enough to leave her home and risk a life of isolation from her people?

The official *flyting* had ended, though onlookers happily took up the challenge of continuing the game amongst themselves—Sitric's men foremost among them. Astrid rose, overwhelmed and exhausted and in need of somewhere quiet to think. She stepped away from the table and took several steps before someone touched her elbow, seeking her attention.

Her first thought was that it was Cormac. Her second was to berate herself over the first. Upon turning around, she discovered it was Finn.

Tall—as were all the Fianna—and blonde with a pleasing face, Astrid couldn't have been happier that this was the man who'd married her cousin. He had a gentle heart and a gentler soul, and he would make a good partner for Eva.

"I don't know what happened." He pitched his voice low.

"He needed training," Astrid replied, matching his tone. "It's my fault."

Finn smiled. "I don't mean tonight. I mean between the two of you. He doesn't tell us anything, but he's grown even quieter of late, his manner more brooding."

"Oh." Astrid didn't know what to say to that. What did he think was going on? Did he believe them to be lovers? Or was he speaking of their bargain?

"I don't know what happened, but I do know he cares for you. He doesn't speak his heart, but his actions say enough."

It was an odd thing to say, even given the circumstances. "His actions?"

"He's been learning *Norrøna*."

Astrid blinked several times, feeling her cheeks warm.

"He came to me and asked me to teach him. He wouldn't say why, but I'd have to be a fool not to guess."

Indeed. "Thank you," she managed. "I had no idea."

"If I know Cormac, he won't tell you until he learns enough to speak it. And don't tell him I said anything—he'd be furious."

"I won't," she promised.

They parted ways, Finn returning to the Fianna and Astrid wandering to her room and collapsing on her bed in a pile of doubt and confusion. That man was learning her language. He was competing in a tournament for her.

And he was coming dangerously close to winning more than just the games.

CHAPTER TWENTY-ONE

U NCERTAINTY TORE AT Astrid as she watched the men walk toward the frothing sea of Dyflin's harbor. Ships with tall masts and colorful cloth sails bobbed like children's toys at the whims of the water. She dreaded today's contest, though it would be a good metric for measuring the men's suitability, at least in any way that mattered to an Ostman. Sailing and swimming were a way of life, necessary skills to seek new lands and go *viking*. The ability to defend oneself in the water held as much import as on land.

The contest appeared simple. The men would dive into the water and swim out toward the first rocks that jutted from the water's surface. The distance was about seven furlongs and not too strenuous, even for someone who hadn't trained at swimming. The trick lay in reaching the stone and returning to the shore safely, for the men were told that it was expected and encouraged to thwart one another along the route. Sitric's men had demonstrated the contest for them this morning and now, as clouds threatened over the harbor, the men stripped off their shirts and prepared to dive into the angry sea. The currents alone would prove a challenge, and that was to say nothing of the other men.

Astrid's gut insisted that she cheer on Cormac, in spite of that kiss. Oh, aye, she'd thought about little else besides that night. The passion she'd found within herself had scared her, bringing to the surface fears she hadn't realized she even held. So while her first instinct was to cheer on her champion and stick to their agreement, her heart warned that she played a dangerous game. Though it may be fun while it lasted, it held the potential to end in disaster. Her mind rode the midline, telling her that either way, she'd need to make a decision and sacrifice one thing or another. Perhaps she could simply jump into the water herself, swim away from here, and avoid a marriage entirely, she mused as the men prepared to start the race.

She identified Cormac in the lineup of swimmers by his broad shoulders, towering height, and the sheer volume of rippling muscle across his back. The men dove fearlessly into the choppy waters and, after but a few strokes, the true contest began.

Sláine sat alongside Sitric and Astrid in a place of honor with the family. Catrin held forth a row behind them, chatting with one of Sitric's guardsmen.

"How are you enjoying your time in Dyflin?" Astrid asked Sláine.

Sitric didn't turn toward them, but the tilt of his head shifted as though he were listening to the conversation.

"It's lovely here," Sláine replied politely, never taking her eyes off the water. "My father's told me so much about it, and about all of you, that I'm so pleased to finally be here and experience it myself."

Astrid followed Sláine's gaze. She couldn't tell which of the swimmers held her attention, but she made a guess nonetheless. "I suppose that you must know Cormac fairly well, and you'd be concerned for his welfare in these games."

Sláine turned to her fully and nodded. "He lived with us as long as I can remember. He's like a son to my father and a brother to me, as are Diarmid and Conan."

"How many children did your father foster?"

"Many," Sláine replied, "as befits a king of his standing. But word spread quickly of how well he did with the children and how much he enjoyed them. Many of his relatives from across Éire sent their sons and daughters to stay with us. It was a wonderful way to grow up, and I had no shortage of friends to play with. But yes, Cormac in particular grew quite close to my father, especially after the falling out. I'm glad that he stayed with us."

The shouts of the crowd drew their attention back to the water. Sláine gasped. Astrid's hand flew to her chest when she saw what had caused the upset.

"They're going to drown him!" Sláine cried.

Astrid watched in horror as Teague and Cairell joined forces against Cormac, no doubt since he posed the greatest threat to their victories. Cormac fought back, but he clearly hadn't expected an attack by both men. First one, and then the other, shoved him by the shoulders until his head was fully submerged.

"It's against the rules to fight two against one," Astrid pleaded with Sitric, all concerns forgotten, save one.

"He'll be fine," Sitric waved a dismissive hand. "Give him a moment and he'll realize all he has to do is break a few rules to get out of it."

Cormac did not strike Astrid as a rule-breaker, but she didn't say as much to her brother. He was under the water for an eternity before he resurfaced, gasping for air.

It was entirely unfair, and her brother should do something. He should interfere. Astrid rose from her seat, the rules breaking and Cormac struggling to breathe. He fought back, just barely surfacing enough to draw a ragged breath.

Her stomach dropped. He might actually lose. He might drown.

And it was all because of her.

The reality of her situation struck her. He was doing this for *her*. He risked his life to help her salvage a losing situation, and all she offered was help endearing Sláine to her brother. Aye, it may have been his words that started her brother down this path to her marrying, but Astrid knew long before that fated dinner that Sitric had her marriage on his mind.

Their exchange of favors fell far short of equal, yet Astrid hadn't truly understood that until this moment. Even if she could somehow ensure that Sitric chose one bride over another, Cormac deserved far greater compensation than what he'd bargained for.

She needed to do something. She could not watch him drown on her account, especially after the way she'd reacted to that kiss. He hadn't deserved that. He had done nothing but support her since his initial blunder. It was time she repaid the favor.

Beside her, the Fianna had gone mad, screaming and shouting.

"Hit them!" Dallan, her cousin, yelled.

Conan echoed the sentiment. "Hit the bastards, Cormac!"

She turned to Sitric, prepared to force her brother's hand—something she had a good bit of experience in—and to throw everything she had into getting her champion safely from the water. At this point, all she cared about was his life.

Just as she opened her mouth to shout some sense into her brother, a fist surfaced from below the water, hitting Cairell square in the jaw and knocking him onto his back with impressive speed. A second blow found Teague, and it quickly turned from a two-against-one drowning to Cormac beating both men senseless, while carefully ensuring they landed on their backs and didn't drown.

Astrid let out a breath she hadn't realized she'd been holding. It looked like he'd decided to break the rules after all. With Teague and Cairell in tow, Cormac somehow managed to swim the rest of the route. He was the last one to return, but he had carried both of his fallen opponents by his side to ensure their survival in the harsh conditions of the harbor. The moment his feet hit the rocky shore, Astrid flew from her seat.

Sitric grabbed her arm, halting her. "Careful," he warned, "that you don't show too much favoritism, or my naming of the champion may be called unfair."

She cast him a sidelong glance. "You'll name Cormac as champion?"

"Provided he continues performing admirably."

"Then why have the contest at all?"

"The point of the contest is to show you that you can find a man with all the qualities you desire, even if he wasn't raised an Ostman, and to get all of your options in the same place so that you can make the best decision."

Astrid chewed on that for a moment. Perhaps her brother hadn't been so foolish and careless with the planning of this tournament as she initially thought. "And you believe I favor Cormac?"

Sitric laughed, a great big bellowing howl that grabbed the attention of everyone in earshot, then he lowered his voice to keep their conversation more private.

Sláine sat between them, smiling to herself and politely ignoring them, though Astrid knew she listened.

"Every time Cormac takes a blow, you flinch," her brother replied. "Every time he delivers one you grin. And you speak with him far more than any of the others. Don't think I haven't noticed how often you angle to have him to yourself."

"He's been here the longest," Astrid defended. "Of course I have more to speak with him about. They've been living with us for months."

"I think he truly cares for you, too," Sitric continued, as though she hadn't argued with him at all. "I noticed about a sennight ago that now, as opposed to the rest of their stay, his face changes when he looks at you."

Astrid felt all the blood rush to her face, her head light as the foam on the surface of the sea. "He pities me, 'tis all," she argued.

Sitric caught her gaze, as he did every time he wanted to ensure she didn't dismiss his words. "You could do a lot worse than the Prince of Connachta. I'd be happy to see you choose him."

That silenced her. Cormac wasn't really competing for her hand, was he? She could hardly tell Sitric that. But now she didn't know what she wanted or how she felt, for her brother had unwittingly hit the nail straight on its head. She could no longer deny that she enjoyed Cormac's company, craved it even, and that she enjoyed his attentions more than she ought. But was that enough for her to allow him to actually be her champion? Could she see herself marrying him when her brother named him the winner?

As much as Astrid wanted to fly over the rock-filled shore and squeeze what life remained out of Cormac in celebration, her brother made a fair point. With restraint that surprised Astrid, she instead wandered back to the guest hall in her brother's holding to await his return. She could speak with him alone there without the appearance of favoritism, as Sitric accused.

The longer she waited, pacing before the central hearth fire, the more anxious she grew. She wrung her hands and debated just what she might say to him. She'd been so worried. Guilt flooded her, followed by frustration. She was furious with herself. She was furious with him for allowing her to make such easy use of him and his skills. Oath of service or not, he shouldn't die simply so that she might avoid an unwanted marriage.

When the doors to the hall burst open, Astrid still hadn't a clue as to what she would say. The Fianna all entered at once, talking and shouting and laughing and surrounding Cormac as he dried off with a strip of cloth in their midst. His shirt, she realized. He used his shirt to dry off, which explained why his torso was still bare.

The conversation died down when they noticed her waiting.

"I say we go have a round of sparring," Conan declared. "Illadan?" He looked to the leader of the Fianna questioningly.

"Absolutely. Fianna, grab your weapons and meet me on the field," Illadan called.

In mere moments, the men were armed with staves and practice swords and headed back out, except for Cormac, who received a sound slap on his back from Diarmid as he passed his brother. Niamh and Cara followed them from the hall, leaving Astrid standing alone before her giant, shirtless champion.

She wanted to run to him.

She wanted to run away.

Instead, she landed somewhere in the middle, standing her ground as he approached her. "What are you doing?" she demanded, wincing at her own poor choice of words. Gods, what a terrible way to start.

But, patient as ever, Cormac took her outburst in stride, his face unreadable. "My best," he answered simply.

Clarity descended with his words, and Astrid finally decided what it was she needed to say to him. Between the kiss and the dangerous swim and the inequality of their agreement, she didn't know where he thought this was headed. Frankly, neither did she.

The more she contemplated it, the more she worried that she, too, may be getting the wrong idea. She couldn't stop thinking about his kiss, about what it might feel like if he pulled her into his arms again. His very bare, very muscular arms, that waited just out of reach.

"But why?" she asked. "Why are you doing your best?"

He took a long, slow step toward her, a storm brewing in his cloudy blue eyes. "Ask me what you really want to know."

A shiver shot straight from her core up her spine. "This agreement isn't fair to you," she continued, ignoring him.

He took another step. The salty scent of the sea wafted from him toward her.

"And you were nearly killed."

Another step.

Her back touched the wall. She should be shouting at him, but no words came out. Her breath faltered and her head spun. He was so close that she could feel the heat of his body against hers. But she wanted him closer.

"Do you actually care for me?" Her question came out so softly she wondered if she'd even spoken it aloud.

Slowly, giving her plenty of opportunity to shy away, his hand reached for her face. She leaned into it, unable to stop herself. His voice broke, sending another rush of excitement through her as he gave his answer.

"Yes."

CHAPTER TWENTY-TWO

HER EYES HADN'T left his lips for the entirety of their conversation, excepting the singular moment when she stared straight at his bare chest and arms. Cormac knew that he played with fire, but that kiss awakened something within him that had slumbered for far too long. And, in spite of her rejection of him the night he'd kissed her, she wasn't running off just yet.

"Do you want me to leave?" he asked, his hands aching to reach for her again.

She shook her head, her full, pouty lips parting beneath his thumb.

He wanted her so badly, but he read her wrong last time. He wasn't going to make that mistake again. "Do you want me to kiss you?"

She bit her lip, testing the limits of his willpower, then nodded her head.

Tilting her chin up, he lowered his lips to hers. The sweet taste of her shattered what little control he had left. The way she melted into him, kissing him back in equal measure, told Cormac that she wanted it as badly as he did.

Her fingers raked over his bare chest, leaving a trail of fire in their wake.

He returned the gesture in kind, his hands devouring her. Everything about her was soft and supple, yet just as fierce as he'd come to expect from the tempestuous princess.

She gasped at his touch. He ached to pick her up and carry

her to his room, to throw her onto his bed and make her his. Instead, he deepened the kiss.

His hands moved over her hips, up the sides of her body until he ran a thumb over her breast, finding a hard nipple and coaxing a moan from her. Maybe he should take her to his room. He shifted, preparing to carry her off.

Someone cleared their throat in the center of the hall.

Astrid gasped, but Cormac could tell from the suppressed laugh that it was his menace of a brother, Conan. Letting his hands fall from the beauty with a beleaguered sigh, he turned and raised a brow.

"Everyone's on their way to the feasting hall. Best we get over there as well." Conan's eyes glittered with amusement but he wisely held his tongue.

Cormac thanked him, watching him leave before turning back to Astrid. He found her honey-hued eyes staring at him from beneath thick, dark lashes, her face flushed and her lips red as berries. He'd never be able to look at her again without imagining her like that.

"You never answered my question the other day. Do you want me to let your Ostman win, princess?"

Her fingers traced the lines of his jaw, her eyes hungry. "Not just yet," she teased in a husky, playful voice. She pulled his face to hers, her fingers putting gentle pressure along his rough jawline, and she planted one more lingering kiss on his lips. "Meet me outside after the hall clears tonight."

Astrid fled the hall, leaving him in shock. She hadn't run off when he admitted his true feelings. Quite the opposite, in fact. Encouraged, Cormac followed after her to join his brothers in the hall, unable to keep a smile from his face.

Cormac entered Sitric's hall to find the contestants more subdued tonight than they had been previously, likely exhausted from their fight to survive in the harbor. Only one or two of the suitors ventured over to Astrid. Cormac couldn't help but feel pleased that Teague and Cairell kept to themselves in a corner, no doubt licking their wounded pride. Servants prepared the tables for the meal while folk finished up their conversations.

"So what was it you were saying about *not* marrying the princess?" Conan greeted him, grinning like a fool.

"As it stands, that's still the plan," Cormac replied.

Conan narrowed his eyes. "It didn't look like the plan."

"She hasn't expressed an interest in it being otherwise."

"Maybe not verbally," Conan taunted.

Diarmid spotted them from their usual seats at Sitric's table and hurried to join them. "Well? What happened?"

Cormac rubbed his neck. "She thanked me for competing."

Conan smacked him—hard—then turned to Diarmid. "He's holding out on you."

"Does that mean you like her now?" Diarmid asked Cormac.

"That's how it looked, aye. Mutual liking," Conan teased.

"Excellent," Diarmid proclaimed, "that means you're in a good mood, then, aye?"

That could only mean trouble. "Why?"

"I know you've been busy, but the tournament is nearly finished, and we've still not spoken to him."

Cormac knew "him" referred to Cahill, as all three of them hesitated to call the man their father. "Let's get this over with," Cormac grumbled.

Though Teague didn't pose a threat to his victory, they still needed to determine what their father hoped to achieve and whether or not he made any progress on it. Cormac led Conan and Diarmid over to where their father skulked near an empty table.

"I wondered when you'd finally come and face me like men," he muttered when they stopped before him.

Diarmid let out a low whistle.

"Hello to you, too," Cormac answered, fighting to stay calm in the presence of the man who'd so easily cast him aside.

"You're lucky none of the women heard you," Conan told him. "I can think of four in this very room who'd love to prove that sentiment wrong."

"Six," Cormac corrected him, recalling that the two brides sent by Brian were spirited enough to take exception to his father's poor choice of greeting.

"I must admit," Cahill began in a condescending tone, the sound of his voice sending Cormac straight back to his childhood, "I understand why Brian would insist Sitric marry his daughter. For reasons of subjugation, of course, and the ostensible keeping of the peace. But I fail to see how having you also marry the sister accomplishes anything further and, if that was indeed his intent, why he didn't simply demand it as part of the agreement?"

"Brian did not ask me to compete," Cormac replied drily.

Cahill raised a wild, bushy brow, the one riven by a jagged scar. "That might lead me to assume you are so inadequate that you must compete for the princess's hand instead of simply asking for it. Not afraid she'd deny you, are you?"

Cormac knew better than to expect civility from his father, yet he'd still dared to hope. "An interesting assessment," he countered, "as you appear to be doing much the same, but with a poorer showing."

Diarmid snickered and Conan grinned. Cormac forced himself to keep a straight face, knowing he'd landed a blow at last on his father. It was a pittance for payback, but it was a start.

"You're quick to disparage your own brother." Cahill nodded toward Teague, sitting beside Cairell in the far corner of the room.

"If you aren't our father, how could he be our brother?" Cormac's mirth disappeared. "Or have you forgotten our last conversation?"

"Why are you here, old man?" Conan interrupted.

Cormac had allowed his emotions to overwhelm his sense— the memory of his father's rejection, of that feeling of being discarded like refuse threatening to swallow him. The moment he stood his ground, he nearly forgot their mission.

"Isn't it obvious? We're here to get Teague a wife."

"You know Sitric cannot choose Teague, no matter his performance. You're a right bastard, but you're no fool. Brian would never allow such an alliance between former and current opponents." Cormac leveled the challenge at his father, laying it all out on the table. He wasn't one to mince words, and he wished to end this conversation as quickly as possible.

Cahill shrugged dramatically. "If the lady desires him, Sitric may not have a choice."

A flicker of rage ignited, and Cormac felt it threatening to burst forth.

Diarmid placed a hand on his shoulder, as though he sensed the change in Cormac. Conan stepped between Cormac and the man who'd once been their father. "The lady's feelings hold no sway in this matter," Conan replied, taking Cormac's place in the conversation. "Sitric knows it would cause trouble that he hasn't the manpower to handle."

Cahill's eyes widened, brightening as he stared over Cormac's shoulder. "Perhaps the lady herself can enlighten us," he called, his voice sickeningly sweet.

They turned to find Astrid eyeing all of them suspiciously. "Perhaps," she allowed tightly.

"We were discussing whether or not political prejudice may play a part in your brother's selection of the victor," Cahill informed her. "I'd hate to see you lose an excellent partner out of malice for his circumstances."

Astrid's narrow nostrils flared, her jaw tightening. "An odd concern for someone who invited themselves to this tournament," she quipped. "You're lucky my brother didn't turn you away the moment you arrived, as I'd have done. I suggest that instead of accusing him of malice, you thank him for his graciousness."

Cahill's gloating turned to fury, darkness flattening his features. Instead of biting back, he bowed to the princess, surprising Cormac.

Astrid, apparently finished with the exchange, turned and

walked away. Cormac couldn't take his eyes off the way her blue dress, the color of a robin's egg in spring, fell enticingly around her narrow hips. His fingers itched to grab them, to pull her toward him. Shaking such foolishness from his head, he forced himself back to the problem of his father allying with Sitric.

Just as he'd predicted from the very beginning, this woman would be the death of him.

CHAPTER TWENTY-THREE

ASTRID WAITED FOR Cormac outside the hall. Butterflies filled her stomach to bursting, as they had of late whenever they were about to meet. She carried an armful of blankets and a spare cloak, in case Cormac didn't have his with him. Though bitter cold gripped the air, it was the first night in a month when the stars shone clearly. On nights like these, when it was so cold you could see your breath before you, sometimes the spirits of the ancestors fought in the skies above and put on a magnificent show for any who dared to seek them out.

It had only happened a handful of times in her life, but that didn't stop Astrid from looking for them at every opportunity. Sitric told her that she was lucky to have seen them at all, as they tended to do battle the most over their homelands far to the north, where the skies were clearer and the nights colder.

"Are we camping?" Cormac asked, shaking her from her thoughts as he approached. Without a word, he grabbed the blankets, carrying them for her with a smile that made her heart pound.

"We're sitting," she corrected.

She led him to a spot not far from their holding. Only a short way down the path into town, the track veered sharply, leading to a clifftop that overlooked the harbor. It afforded an unimpeded view of the ships below them and the sea beyond. She and Sitric both enjoyed going there from time to time.

Cormac laid the blankets on the ground, sitting on them and

reaching for her with both arms—a clear invitation for her to sit in his lap. Against her better judgment, she accepted. She leaned against his hard body, soaking up the warmth.

"My brother and I both like it here," she mumbled, desperately trying to break the tension that grew between them.

"I can see why," he whispered back. The heat from his breath washed over her ear and tickled her neck. "It's beautiful. And thank you for coming to my rescue again earlier," he added, his chin settling on her shoulder.

"It's the least I could do. You've been coming to my rescue for weeks now, and I didn't realize until today just how much you risked to do so."

His arms squeezed tighter around her, pulling her into the warmth of his chest. She leaned her head back, letting herself enjoy the closeness.

A light appeared on the horizon, at the far edge of this inky sky. A green streak, the color of saplings in spring, flashed from it, dancing like a serpent. The light cracked overhead again, this time reaching further, a flame sputtering atop a candle. A second light appeared beside it, this one stronger. As it reached toward them across the darkness, it changed from an eerie green to the same blushing pink as an autumn apple. The two lights danced above them like waves in the sky.

"I've not seen them since I was a boy still living in the north," Cormac whispered, his voice filled with awe.

"They don't visit us often here, but whenever a night is clear and cold, I try to go out and check."

"What do you think they are?"

His question didn't surprise her in the least, given his pensive nature. "My parents told me they're the spirits of our ancestors fighting battles of old."

"They don't get to rest when they die?"

The shock in his voice made her chuckle. "Is that what you'd really want? To do nothing forever?" She felt his shoulders shrug behind her, his arms somehow wrapping her even tighter.

"I hadn't really thought about it," he replied. The smile in his voice coaxed out one of her own. "What do you call them?"

"*Norðrljós*. The Northern Lights."

His lips brushed the bare skin of her neck. "And what do you call this?"

"*Hals*," she breathed, tilting her head to allow him better access.

"Mmm." The low hum vibrated against her collarbone. He pushed her dress off her shoulder, his soft lips following. "And this?"

She leaned against him, pressing as hard as she could. "*Djarfr*," she smiled. "Which means bold."

He stilled. "Too bold?"

Astrid turned in his lap, facing him. She felt possessed by some sort of spirit, hardly able to breathe let alone think. She didn't *know* anything—she *felt* everything. Her hands ran down the broad lines of his shoulders, his chest. "Maybe not bold enough."

He pulled her lips to his with a hungry growl. Their kiss yesterday had been passionate. This kiss was explosive.

It ignited a fire that left her throbbing and dizzy. She slipped her hands beneath his shirt, her fingers following the hard planes of his body downward to the hem of his trews.

He inhaled sharply, his eyes clouding over. With painful slowness, he unfastened her dress. His gaze raked over her, scorching, before he devoured her lips once more.

The air bit her naked skin. She shivered at the shock of the cold, but she was too far gone to stop now. She ached for him. She needed him. She wanted him. Her hand grasped the hard length between them, exploring.

Cormac groaned, a deep, throaty sound that only made her shiver more—this time, though, it wasn't from cold. He braced them with his arms, laying her back on the blanket and covering her with his body. His hands caressed her legs, bunching her dress toward her waist as he found the part of her that ached for him.

His fingers circled and teased, until Astrid squirmed in frustration. Then he sank them inside her.

Astrid gasped at the sensation, the delicious pressure. For a moment she thought that would be it. Then he moved. And all she wanted was *more*. "Cormac," she breathed.

In response, his hand continued its work and his lips found her nipples. Sucking, nipping, working her into a need so desperate she would do anything to have it filled.

"Please," she begged, tugging his trews open. She took him in hand, guiding him to where she craved him. "Please."

At last, he obliged, entering her slowly and taking her breath away.

"More," she demanded. "Cormac, I want more." Astrid lifted her hips, taking in as much of him as she could. She felt so full, so complete. And, somehow, still wanting.

Everything faded to a blur of pressure and pleasure and the man who gave it to her. Under the flickering lights of stars and spirits they moved together, until Astrid no longer knew where she ended and Cormac began. A pressure, an urgency built inside her, demanding, begging. But for what, she did not know.

He drove into her harder and harder, both of them gasping for breath as they joined. A noise of pure ecstasy escaped him as he pulled her close to him, the look on his face and the feel of him inside her shattering the world around her.

Her eyes squeezed shut. She held onto him as though he would keep her from falling apart. It felt as though time stopped altogether, leaving only the two of them on the cliffs under the dancing sky.

When she opened her eyes again, she searched Cormac's expectant face. And what she saw there scared her into action, for the only word she could use to describe it was 'love.' And she wasn't ready to think about that just yet.

He helped her back into her dress, wrapping her in blankets as she settled back in his lap, her head resting once more on his strong chest, his arms holding her tight. That had been amazing, magical. But she had let her feelings run wild, and she wasn't entirely certain she'd made the right decision. Everything felt so right with Cormac, which terrified her all the more.

"I've been thinking about your problem," he whispered as they gazed up at the twinkling stars. "I have another idea."

"It's almost certainly better than anything I've come up with," she smiled. "Tell me, then. What do I try next with my brother?"

"Tell him you choose me."

She sat up, looking at him over her shoulder in confusion. Hadn't that been their plan all along? "And then?"

His throat worked over the words. "And then marry me."

"But," she stammered, "you can only marry for love."

"Aye." His eyes silently pleaded with her.

Astrid's stomach dropped. He loved her. That was what he was saying. And he wanted to *actually* marry her. She felt as though she'd swallowed her tongue, a familiar panic descending over her.

Cormac took her hands in his. "Without fear, there is no courage," he whispered, somehow reading her mind.

She wanted to make him happy, to say what he wanted to hear. But her mind went blank in the face of her terror. "I'm too afraid."

CHAPTER TWENTY-FOUR

HE'D MADE A huge mistake.

Of course one evening of fooling around wouldn't change the way she felt about him. Or, rather, it wouldn't change the way she thought about him. She clearly felt the same desire that he did for her, but Cormac wasn't so naive that he believed desire and love to be the same. He could see it in her face, that she even now searched for a way to let him down without hurting him overmuch. What a fool he'd been. He, of all people, should have known better. She'd been more than clear of her expectations.

She didn't want a husband.

She chose him because she knew he would refuse the marriage, and now he'd gone and made a mess of it. Ignoring the ache in his chest, he decided to cut his losses and spare both of them any further embarrassment.

"We could actually wed," he continued, cursing himself the entire time, "and if you wish to stay in Dyflin with your family, you'd be free to do so. We could have a marriage in name so that you could keep living the life that you want."

The lights continued dancing above them, but the woman in his arms had long since claimed Cormac's attention.

"I couldn't do that to you." She shook her head, tresses the color of coals in a fire brushed his face as she turned to look at him. "I like you a lot, Cormac, and I would be lucky to marry you—any woman would. But you deserve someone who can't wait to leave their home and follow you back to Brian's kingdom. Don't waste your marriage of love on me."

On someone who couldn't love him back, was what she meant. His throat clenched. Understanding stabbed him like a knife in the gut, but he'd already laid it all before her, so he may as well press on.

"It could only be you, Astrid," he whispered, hating the truth in his words and wishing it weren't so. "And if I could give you the life you wish, it wouldn't be a waste."

"I'll think on it," she promised, "but we should probably head back. It's getting late, and tomorrow will be difficult."

"What's tomorrow?" He grasped onto the change of subject.

"*Glíma.*"

He had no idea what that meant. He raised a questioning brow, tilting his head.

"Wrestling," she explained. "It's much like *knattleikr*, but without the ball and stick."

That sounded like a difficult day, indeed. Though Cormac had no doubt he'd be able to best Teague and Cairell, Astrid was correct that he would need his strength and rest to do so. Collecting the blankets, they walked side by side in silence back to the holding. She bid him a tentative goodnight when they parted, each going to their own halls, but her eyes didn't meet his again.

When Cormac entered the guest hall, he found Diarmid, Conan, and Cara sitting in the nearest alcove on fur-covered couches. Cara held a giant book in her hands, its pages gilded with brilliant illumination visible even from Cormac's perch in the doorway. Cara loved to read, and she especially loved that book—the one that Diarmid had given her as a gift just before their betrothal.

Normally, Cormac would head straight to his room to be alone and digest what had just happened, but Astrid's response had thoroughly gutted him. The quiet warmth of the hall soothed his damaged heart. Perhaps this time he could find more comfort in company rather than solitude. And so, in a decidedly uncharacteristic fashion, he walked over, taking a seat beside Conan and across from Cara and Diarmid.

His brothers stared at him expectantly, having ceased their conversation when he entered.

"Are you really going to make us ask?" Conan whined beside him.

"Are you really going to make me tell you?" Cormac grumbled.

"That bad, huh? What happened?" Diarmid leaned forward, propping his elbows on his legs.

"I told her I'd marry her. She said she'd think about it."

Diarmid cringed. "That's pretty bad."

"What are you going to do?" Conan asked.

Cormac sighed. "I'm in it now. I don't have much choice but to keep going. The deal was that I win and then refuse to marry her, even though I think that's a terrible plan. But if that's what she wants, that's what I'll do."

"Maybe you should try talking with her again tomorrow," Conan suggested. "Perhaps she'll think on it and change her mind by morning."

Cara slammed her book shut, her lips thinning in irritation as she looked first at Diarmid and then at Conan.

"Something you wish to say, dear?" Diarmid teased.

Cormac had never quite understood their relationship. They were even more opposite one another than he and Astrid. He loved his brother despite their differences, and Cara appeared to feel much the same, so he hadn't really questioned it. Watching them together, though, provided endless entertainment, even on a night like tonight when he felt so despondent.

"I cannot sit here and listen to you give him such horrid advice." She turned to Cormac. "If Astrid says she'll think on it, then that's what she'll do. If you're desperate for a complete rejection, then by all means, ask her again tomorrow."

"Then what advice would you give?" Cormac asked.

"Give her time." Cara's tone softened. "Even if she cares for you, that's a big decision. It will change her life in every conceivable way, and she wasn't prepared to marry in the first place. I'd have said much the same in her position, even if I did like you and even if I may eventually agree to a marriage."

"It's true." Diarmid nodded, shooting his betrothed a playful look. "She denied my first proposal outright by betrothing herself to another man, so," he shrugged, "it could have gone worse for you, I suppose."

Cormac stared agape at his brother, shaking his head. "I can't believe I'm saying this, but that does somehow make me feel better."

Conan stood, walking past Cormac on his way to bed. "Keep after her." His hand fell hard on Cormac's shoulder in solidarity. "But without bothering her, as Cara said."

"Clear as a cloudy sky," Cormac quipped with more amusement than he felt. "Thank you."

"You can do it," Diarmid agreed, offering his hand to Cara and leading her out of the alcove. Cara smiled at him encouragingly.

Cormac sat alone, listening to the crackling fire in the center of the room. He felt better and worse all at once. The part of the night with Astrid had been so magical, like they had a real connection, like she was finally letting him in. Like maybe she felt the same.

Then he'd opened his mouth and that horrible conversation had come out. That had felt like the end of everything, a dagger straight to his heart. After speaking with his brothers and Cara, he didn't know what to think. And the idea of waiting only made him feel worse.

CHAPTER TWENTY-FIVE

A STRID'S NERVES REACHED a breaking point as she took her place beside her brother and Sláine on the side of the tournament field. She'd laid awake the entire night wrestling with her own fears. She wanted to accept Cormac's proposal, but she still hadn't decided whether she would. What her heart wanted and what her mind told her was right were two entirely different things, and the battle between them yet persisted.

He'd offered to let her stay in Dyflin—the thing she'd wanted the most, a place that felt like home with people who understood her and welcomed her. But he deserved better than an absent wife and a wasted marriage. He deserved a woman who wanted to go with him, who wanted nothing but him.

The only decision she'd reached was that if she accepted his proposal, she would leave Dyflin with him, which was the source of her entire dilemma.

The point of this farce with Cormac had been to devise a way to keep her at home. The point of choosing him as her champion had been to keep her in a place where she belonged. Her greatest fear was moving somewhere she would be eyed with constant suspicion and misunderstanding, expected to turn and attack at any moment as her forebears had done.

She had but one question left to answer: Did she love Cormac enough to leave her home?

"I had an interesting conversation with Cahill last night." Sitric's ice blue eyes glittered with mischief as he interrupted her thoughts. "It seems he was told by a certain princess that Teague needn't even bother competing, as he won't be winning."

Astrid scoffed. "That is *not* what I said."

Her brother's eyes narrowed knowingly.

"Well, not in so many words," she amended. "I suppose it could have been implied."

Sitric's grin only broadened. "Does that mean you've chosen your champion, then?"

Astrid's heart thudded in agreement. Gods, yes, she'd chosen him, but her mind and her heart remained at odds. "I leave it to you," she told him. "Choose the man you believe to be best."

Her brother would do just that, though it brought a sickening feeling to her stomach that she hadn't simply elected Cormac outright. She still had time, too, for the men were only beginning to take up their positions and pair off for the wrestling matches. As with all of the other events at the tournament, the men who had thrown the smallest stones would compete first, working up to the strongest of her champions, which meant that Cormac would be the last to wrestle in each round.

As the first two men squared off, flicking an arm here and sliding a hand there to taunt the other, someone tapped on Astrid's shoulder from behind her. Turning, she was surprised to find Cahill.

"I wondered if I might have a word with you, my lady."

Astrid cast a quick glance at her brother, who was deep in conversation with the beautiful Sláine. Smiling to herself, Astrid rose. At least she'd done something right for Cormac—it looked as though her brother had finally chosen his bride.

As happy as that thought made Astrid, the prospect of a conversation with Cahill soured her mood. She had no love lost for the man who'd clearly wounded Cormac and had sacked her home.

"My brother tells me the truth in my words last night distressed you," she opened boldly.

Cahill didn't fluster in the least at her accusation. "My intuition tells me that you intend to wed my son."

"I'm not marrying Teague," she replied quickly. Too quickly.

A small, cold smile spread across Cahill's face. "It is not of Teague that I speak."

Astrid despised this entire conversation, and it had only just begun. How could he disown Cormac yet continue to claim him as a son? How could he show such support to only half of his children and still show his face to the others, as though he hadn't wounded them all deeply?

"How must it feel, I wonder, to have your own father reject you, even when you do all in your power to please him?" she mused aloud.

"Betraying an oath would please no man," he replied coldly, "especially a father."

"He was a child then, as any adult would understand."

"You defend him admirably. When your marriage to him fails, you're welcome to inquire about a union with Teague. I could use someone with your standards of loyalty."

Astrid took exception to that comment, ignoring his implication that she should wed first one son, then the other. "And why would you assume my marriage to Cormac might fail?" She felt her temper rising, the blood pounding in her veins at an alarming pace.

"My son is loyal to Brian to a fault," he answered evenly. "I suspect the same is not true for you, and I also suspect that there is great potential in the future for that to cause some dissent between you. Should your brother and Brian have a falling out, who would you support—your husband or your brother?"

Astrid didn't like a single word that had left his lips since she'd met him, but these words she despised most of all, for they ignited a fear that had laid dormant within her. Perhaps this was her true hesitation, and she simply hadn't been able to put the words to it.

"You're a loving father," she hissed, "to plant the seeds of doubt in a bride before the wedding."

"I would hate for you to go through the heartbreak of losing someone you love to Brian," he remarked. "It's a sentiment I've had to accept over the years, and I'd hate to see the same fate befall you." He took his leave abruptly, apparently having said what he'd come to say.

Astrid returned to her seat beside Sláine and Sitric. Even knowing Cahill had set out to drive her and Cormac apart, his words settled in the pit of her stomach. She'd meant everything she'd said to Cahill. It filled her with grief and anger on Cormac's behalf that he'd had to choose between his father and his foster father at such a young and impressionable age. All she wanted was to see him loved and happy now, as he deserved back then, and to get past all of this nonsense with his father.

Astrid took several deep breaths while the realization sank in. Rather than driving them apart, Cahill's comments solidified Astrid's decision. She turned to Sitric, interrupting his conversation with Sláine.

"Cormac," she told him firmly, her decision made. "You should choose Cormac."

CHAPTER TWENTY-SIX

CORMAC HANDILY BESTED Cairell in the first round of wrestling, and then his brother in the second. It didn't shock him in the least, for he'd bested them numerous times over the course of the games already. His fate with Astrid was of far greater concern to him than his opponents in the tournament.

He was terrified that she would deem him just as inadequate as his father had. He hoped that she'd choose him because she actually loved him, and not because he was the best option she had at present. Halfway through slamming Teague into the muddy ground, he realized the entire affair was out of his hands. He'd moved his pieces on the board and now he awaited her decision.

When all the matches had finished, Sitric called the men over to where he and Astrid, along with Sláine and Gormla, sat on the sidelines.

"It seems we have finally run out of ale!" he shouted, pausing while the crowd roared in laughter. "And as you all know by now, that means it's time for our games to be at their end.

"First and foremost, I would like to thank you all for making this such an enjoyable *Jól* holiday season."

A round of applause followed that, and many in the crowd mirrored the king's sentiments.

"I would also like to thank you for traveling so far and fighting so hard to win my sister's hand in marriage. Unfortunately, I can only marry her off once, but each and every one of you deserves a happy life with a beautiful wife for your efforts."

Another round of applause and shouts of agreement rippled through the crowd.

"For this tournament and this wife, I have decided upon the victor. Cormac O'Conor, champion and foster son of King Brian Boru of Mumhain, son of King Cahill of Connachta, congratulations on your victory."

Cormac's head spun. It took several moments for Sitric's statement to sink in and become rational thought. In front of Cormac, the Fianna cheered louder than anyone else. They made a ruckus that shook the heavens, but Cormac couldn't celebrate. Not just yet.

For it was no victory at all if it didn't come with Astrid.

He could hardly breathe as he watched her walk across the field. When her eyes met his, a smile brightened her face. He didn't know what to expect; his skin tingling like the pricks of a thousand needles. When she reached him, she threw her arms around his neck, pulling him into an embrace that elicited another round of cheers from the Fianna and from a good many of the onlookers in the crowd, too.

"A well-earned victory," she congratulated him softly. Pulling away, she cupped his face between her hands, running her thumbs over his cheeks. "I will marry you, and I am so sorry that I didn't say as much yesterday."

Cormac's cheeks stretched across his face, completely beyond his control.

She loved him. She actually loved him.

He knew her well enough now to know that she wouldn't have agreed if she didn't really want him. Astrid never had trouble standing up for herself and speaking her mind.

She pulled his face to hers, kissing him like no one else was there. Her lips pressed hard against his as her arms entwined around his neck. Cormac drank her in, running his hand through her silky red hair.

Cheers rippled through the crowd, only this time the raucous didn't bother Cormac in the least. If his lips weren't otherwise occupied, he'd have cheered right along with them. Because he'd won the heart of the woman he loved, and that was worth celebrating.

"Congratulations!" Cahill shouted over the noise of the crowd. "What a fine showing, and what a well-earned victory indeed!" He stepped forward, so that he stood halfway between Sitric and Cormac, looking between the two of them as he spoke.

Cahill's suspicious behavior set Cormac on edge. His father had hoped for an alliance, by marriage if necessary, and he wasn't getting one now. Why was he putting on such a good-natured show?

"Thank you," Cormac answered him. "It was well-done by all."

"You'll be married soon, I imagine?" Cahill asked. "A wedding seems the perfect ending to the *Jól* festivities."

"We hadn't—" Astrid began, but Sitric strode over to take up the conversation.

"I agree, it would be perfect. What say you, sister, shall we end the tournament with a wedding?"

"You'll have to wait a few days, won't you?" Cahill turned to Sitric. "For the family to arrive."

"Why are you being so nice?" Astrid asked, stealing the words from Cormac's mind.

He'd never ask them aloud, of course, but he appreciated her boldness.

"Astrid," Sitric tsked. "Cahill has been nothing but pleasant this past month."

Astrid didn't look the least bit remorseful, still glaring openly at Cahill.

"I am grateful to have had the opportunity to meet with my sons again," Cahill told her. "I hope that this tournament has gotten us started on the path to a better relationship."

That was absolute drivel, and yet it made Cormac's chest swell with hope. He had no love lost for his father after all these years, but it would be good to put the past behind them.

"A midwinter wedding it is!" Sitric declared. "I'll send a messenger to Caiseal to inform Brian and Dunla. I'm certain they'll want to attend."

Cormac couldn't help but smile at that. "Aye, they certainly will."

Even after exchanging something dangerously close to a pleasant conversation with his father, Cormac couldn't shake the feeling that something was off. As they walked back to Sitric's holding, he chewed on his worries until he'd narrowed it down to the wedding.

More likely than not, he was anxious at the prospect of a wedding where his father and Brian were both guests. The last one had not gone well at all.

Aye, that was it, he decided. It was just his own nerves threatening to get the better of him. Putting the matter to rest, he pulled Astrid into a hug while they walked.

This was everything he had worked for, more than he had hoped for, even. How could he be so lucky? He squeezed her tighter against him, letting his cheek rest on the top of her head and forgetting that the rest of the world existed. Now that he had Astrid, what could possibly go wrong?

CHAPTER TWENTY-SEVEN

A SENNIGHT LATER, Brian was due in Dyflin and Cahill had overstayed his welcome. Unfortunately, neither could be changed. Cahill stayed for his son's wedding, a privilege no one could argue over. And she couldn't avoid Brian forever. She knew all along that she would have to face the reality of marrying a man sworn to Brian. She understood that would be the next bridge for her to cross. She had simply not anticipated facing it so soon.

Knowing that Brian could arrive at any time created tension for Cormac and his brothers, who worried over what might transpire between him and Cahill. They'd formed something of a truce with Teague, who appeared interested in getting to know the three brothers he'd left behind in childhood.

Astrid hardly spent a moment apart from Cormac. Even when he trained with the Fianna, she would sit beside Niamh and Cara to watch the men spar in the field they'd taken over for their training. Catrin joined them once or twice, now that it was clear Sitric favored Sláine for his wife.

Late one fog-filled morning, Brian arrived with an entourage fit for a king. Looking upon the line of horses and carriages and carts that made up the king's retinue, Astrid wondered if he'd brought the whole of Caiseal with him. Even at his advanced age, Brian rode atop his horse instead of inside the carriages which bore some of the women of the court.

On horseback beside him was a young man—a boy, really—

whom Astrid didn't recognize. His hair was cut short, not even reaching his shoulders. He had pale brown locks and a thin, though not displeasing, face. Just as Astrid wondered who the boy might be, her mother shot like an arrow from a bow straight toward him. Astrid chuckled aloud at the look of horror on Brian's face when Gormla charged them, but it was gone as quick as it came, softening when he realized where she was headed. The boy must be Astrid's half-brother, Duncan.

Her mother had seen Duncan many times since she'd left Caiseal all those years ago. Even Sitric had met him on the occasions when he'd gone to visit Brian, but Astrid had never made that particular journey and therefore had not yet met her brother, who must be at least fourteen summers. Duncan beamed at their mother, hopping off his horse and straight into her waiting arms. The two of them bent their heads together like a pair of thieves, ready to go sneaking off. Without even sparing a glance at Brian or any of the other guests, Gormla whisked young Duncan off to the feasting hall. The only words that Astrid caught of their conversation involved bread and ships.

The doors on the first carriage opened and a tall woman, thin with dark hair and a round face, stepped out. She wore a regal dress of red and gold, leading Astrid to believe that she must be Queen Dunla, Brian's most recent wife and Cormac's elder sister.

After Dunla, a woman Astrid hadn't dared expect to see alighted from the carriage—her cousin Eva. All sense of propriety fled. Astrid and Eva squealed like children, rushing toward one another and embracing.

"Are you trying to steal my wife?" Finn teased, waiting patiently for Astrid to release Eva into his waiting arms.

"She's always been mine, bard," Astrid shot back with a smile. "I knew her first."

"Aye, but I know her better."

Eva blushed bright pink, smacking Finn on the arm and shaking her head.

"I see that I'm all but forgotten now." Dallan walked over

pulling his sister into a gentle hug and releasing her. "You look well," he smiled. "The journey must have agreed with you."

Eva worried her bottom lip. Everyone stared at her, and the longer they waited for an answer, the more Astrid suspected that her cousin had a secret.

"Eva," Astrid demanded.

"I need to speak with Niamh first," she blurted out.

"Wait." Finn placed a hand on her shoulder, clearly putting it all together.

"You're with child?" Dallan shouted.

Astrid couldn't tell if he was shocked, happy, or horrified. Likely he was all of those and then some.

Eva couldn't keep the smile off her face or the glow off her cheeks. "I think so," she laughed. "Either that or I'm dying. I've hardly been able to keep anything down for weeks now."

Finn fell straight into the role of protector. Before Astrid could even congratulate her cousin, Finn took Eva's hand and started hauling her toward Niamh. "Let's go get you some herbs. Niamh will know what to do. Niamh!"

They all had a good laugh at Finn's antics and the excitement of a baby. It occurred to Astrid then that now that she was marrying Cormac, she'd be able to see her cousins regularly. She'd be there for the birth of Eva's child. One day, perhaps, their children would play together. Smiling to herself at that happy thought, Astrid helped everyone settle into their guest rooms before heading to the hall to discuss the terms of the betrothal. It was the part of the wedding she looked forward to least, as it provided the greatest opportunity for something to go wrong.

Astrid entered the feasting hall to find Cormac, Brian, Dunla, and Sitric waiting. Cormac introduced her to Dunla, a warm, likeable woman with poise and a quiet sort of strength. Astrid could tell from the few words they shared and the way she carried herself that it took a great deal to shake the Queen of Mumhain. She reminded Astrid of Cormac in that way.

They had just sat down to begin when the doors opened and

Cahill entered the hall.

Brian stood right back up, his face outraged. "What's he doing here?"

"Are you suggesting I shouldn't be a part of my own son's marriage contract?"

Oh, Gods. Astrid felt in her bones that this would only get worse, but like a runaway horse with a cart, all she could do was watch.

"You disowned him fourteen years ago!" Brian shouted. "Now that there's money involved, suddenly you're his father again?"

"Is it true?" Sitric asked calmly, stepping in as mediator. "Did you disown him?"

"Publicly," Cormac declared.

Astrid exhaled. There, that should put the matter to rest.

"I'm afraid you'll have to leave, Cahill," Sitric told him.

"You would side with him after all our discussions?" Cahill pressed.

Uh oh. Astrid's pulse quickened. This was taking a very bad turn.

Brian turned on Sitric. "*Discussions?* Have you been meeting with this traitor behind my back?"

"No!" Sitric cried, glaring at Cahill. "He entered his son in the tournament we just held. That's all."

"That and our discussions of alliance." Cahill took a step backward toward the door. "You were open to speaking of it, even if you weren't ready to commit." Turning on his heel, Cahill strode angrily from the hall, leaving chaos in his wake.

"You hosted my enemy," Brian hissed. "You met with him to discuss an alliance, against me, no doubt. You allowed him the chance to make an alliance of marriage through his son." The king's face reddened more with each statement. "You are a traitor."

"Take care with your words," Sitric warned. "I will not stand to be called a traitor when I have betrayed no one."

Everything was falling apart before her eyes—her greatest

fears come to life. Beside her, Cormac looked just as uncomfortable as she felt. He stood, but didn't interrupt. It wasn't their place, and they both knew it. This argument was between her brother and Brian, and nothing they said or did would end it until it had run its course.

"No?" Brian narrowed his furious eyes. "You allowed one of my greatest enemies to remain in your city when you knew I was coming here. How do I know this isn't a trap set to rid you both of your shared burden of the King of Mumhain?"

Sitric's fists came down on the table, sending the cups of ale clattering. "I will not be called traitor. I have hosted your men. I have given my hostage. I have given my oath. And I have sworn to marry your daughter. You will pay the honor price for slander."

"I am finished coddling you like a child," Brian growled. "Either you are my oathsworn or you are a traitor."

"I already swore my oath!" Sitric roared. "And you continue to slander me, in public, no less. You owe me the honor price."

"I'll not be fined for telling the truth," Brian countered, taking a dangerous step toward her brother.

Astrid shot from her seat. "Sitric!" she shouted, trying to get his attention. It was of no use.

His eyes fixed on Brian. "Then I demand an honor duel. We will know then who is telling the truth."

"Sitric, this is madness!" Astrid cried. "There's no need—"

"I accept your duel."

This could not be happening. Curse these men and their inflated senses of honor and ego.

"Excellent," Sitric replied more calmly. "Name your champion. I fight in my own stead, to prove to you the veracity of my claim."

Brian turned toward Cormac, his intent clear.

Astrid forgot how to breathe. This could not be happening. It couldn't.

Cormac grimaced, giving Astrid a pained look. "I will fight as his champion, as my oath demands."

CHAPTER TWENTY-EIGHT

O F ALL THE paths their betrothal negotiations could have taken, beginning with accusations of treachery and ending in a duel was not one that had crossed his wildest imaginings. Cormac only hoped it wasn't too late to convince Astrid that this still could work, that it needn't drive a wedge between them, and that their divided loyalties could be conquered. He held no doubt in his mind that together they could find some way for this to work. How, he still hadn't determined, but it was a question to which he desperately sought the answer.

The look of betrayal on her face concerned him far more than the threat of fighting in any duel. He knew how to best an opponent with his sword, but he couldn't fathom how to convince Astrid that his loyalty to Brian needn't be the end of their relationship.

They left the hall en masse, Brian and Sitric leading the way out toward the field where the Fianna trained every afternoon. The betrothal hung in the air, unfinished in the face of the argument that had just broken out. Cormac was not surprised that Brian took exception to Cahill's presence in Dyflin, nor was he surprised that Sitric took exception to Brian's belligerent choice of words. Both men had tempers. Both lived their lives to the fullest in every way, including defending their own honor. In some ways, the two kings were more alike than they appeared at a glance.

Sitric's men fetched a cloak measuring three meters and laid it in the center of the training field. They hammered hazel staves into the corners, three feet further out. While Cormac had never witnessed a duel in the Ostman manner, he was familiar enough with the concept of a duel to recognize that they set up the field of combat. As he stood there watching, he spied Astrid's blazing hair, the same scarlet red as the paint on the shields the men now laid at each end of the square.

She stormed over to him, her honey eyes lit like amber torches, her expression beautiful and furious all at once.

"Astrid, let me explain," he began.

"Swear to me that you won't kill my brother," she interrupted.

He took a breath, long and deep. He couldn't have a conversation with her while she worried over her brother's life, and so first he addressed the fear he heard in her voice. "The combat is to the surrender, not the death," he assured her. "Your brother's life is safe."

"I don't just mean today."

Cormac took a step back, her words sinking like a stone in his gut. He wanted to tell her he wouldn't. He wanted to assure her that he would never harm her family. But he knew, especially after today, that if Brian battled Sitric again, there was a good chance he would face the King of Dyflin across the battlefield. And as much as he wanted to ease all of her worries, he also wouldn't make a vow that he knew he couldn't keep. Instead, he replied with his own request.

"Swear to me he won't betray Brian."

Astrid's bluster fell away, her silence engulfing the narrow space between them. Astrid didn't often fall silent. More than anyone he'd ever met, she always had something to say, always had a word to get in. That fire was one of the things he loved so much about her, and its absence now was surely a bad sign.

"I don't want to fight Sitric," he told her. He took a step toward her, hoping to close the distance physically if he couldn't bridge the gap with his words.

Astrid retreated. "I can't betray my brother," she whispered.

"I can't marry someone who would destroy my family." She turned on her heels and walked over to join the gathering onlookers.

His gut roiled, his stomach threatening to evict what little he'd eaten so far that day. A burning pain filled the back of his throat, making it difficult to swallow as he watched her walk away from him.

She'd left him.

Cormac grappled with the reality of her words, with how quickly she'd discarded him. Perhaps she never really loved him at all. He'd been a fool for imagining she could. Hadn't that been their bargain from the beginning, that their marriage would never happen? His feelings for her were doomed from the start, yet he'd been too blinded by his attraction to her.

He made his way to one end of the square, numbness overtaking him. He could hardly hold two thoughts together, and he could think of little but the pain he felt at her loss. As Sitric took his place opposite Cormac, one of the guardsmen of Dyflin stepped toward them, addressing the crowd at large.

"The challenger defends first," he announced, gesturing to Sitric. "When the shields are gone, the men have only their swords to defend themselves. The fight continues until one man yields. The first man to yield loses the duel and owes the honor price of three marks of silver to the winner."

Sitric grabbed the first of his three shields from beside the square, drawing his sword and facing Cormac with a grim nod. It was one of the few times Cormac had ever seen his face without a smile—a sentiment he well understood, for he felt much the same. He wanted to battle Sitric as much as he wanted to fight his own brother. But Brian was the reason that he was here. Brian was the reason that he had any family at all. He was the reason that Cormac knew what it meant to be a man of honor, and he wasn't going to let him down, no matter how deeply it wounded him.

Gritting his teeth against the ache in his chest, Cormac picked up a shield and drew his sword, charging the King of Dyflin.

CHAPTER TWENTY-NINE

ASTRID COULDN'T TAKE her eyes off the horrific sight before her: the man she loved fighting the brother she loved. She didn't want to watch either man fall, but she couldn't look away. Even in duels to the first blood, men could be maimed or killed. In a fight to the yield, the risk of serious injury only grew.

Beside her, Brian gripped the narrow arms of the chair that had been brought for him, his knuckles white as he watched the men. On his other side next to Dunla, his daughter Sláine sat, looking similarly conflicted.

Cormac struck first as the defender of Brian's honor. His sword came down on Sitric's shield, shattering it in one mighty blow. Splinters painted the color of blood flew across the field, scattering at the men's feet. Cormac backed up, lifting his own shield to prepare for the blow that would follow from Sitric.

Astrid thought she might be sick. She knew in her heart that Cormac was the greater warrior, but that thought did little to comfort her. Instead, it only increased her concern for her brother. Cormac was a good man and wouldn't deliberately hurt Sitric, but accidents happened.

Sitric fought admirably, striking back and breaking Cormac's shield in turn.

How could she love both of these men? She scooted to the edge of her seat. How could this ever work? She felt ripped in two as she watched Cormac break another of Sitric's shields, the two men she loved most in the world battling before her. Back and forth they went, broken shield after broken shield littering the ground with red.

When finally Sitric ran out of shields, he defended a blow from Cormac with his sword, but it glanced off at an odd angle, cutting into his shoulder and causing him to cry out.

Astrid turned to grab her mother, who no doubt suffered alongside her, but her mother wasn't there. Why would she not be at this duel? She'd gone to the hall with Duncan. Astrid grew more and more confused as she considered her mother's whereabouts.

She tore her gaze from the duel long enough to scour the crowd. Eva and Finn stood behind her and Brian, as did Dallan and Niamh. Cara and Diarmid stood beside Conan, all three of their faces stricken with concern as they watched.

"Have you seen my mother?" she asked Eva over her shoulder.

Her cousin frowned, searching the crowd herself. "I haven't. Not since we arrived."

Brian turned, listening to their conversation.

"I'll go look for her," Niamh offered, her golden braids swaying as she hurried back toward the halls.

Out of the corner of her eye, Astrid saw Brian cast a frantic gaze about the field—not at the duel, but at the onlookers.

He turned toward her, his eyes wild, his face paler than normal. "Cahill isn't here," he said under his breath. "Neither is Teague."

Astrid's stomach lurched as realization settled. "Duncan," she breathed. "Duncan isn't here either."

Niamh raced toward them, panting and shaking her head. She'd apparently sprinted the entire way. "I can't find her," she heaved. "I checked the whole estate."

Sitric cried out when Cormac's blade bit his skin.

Astrid leapt from her seat. "Stop!"

Their swords met again and again. They hadn't heard her.

Cormac raised his sword.

"Hold! Stop!" She screamed, running toward them.

Cormac and Sitric both froze midswing.

"Halt!" Brian called, following Astrid across the field.

Upon hearing Brian's command, Cormac nodded to Sitric, who returned the gesture. They lowered their weapons to the ground.

Astrid's heart hammered painfully as she and Brian closed the distance to the men.

"What's happened?" Sitric asked, his brows knitting in concern.

"Astrid, what's wrong?" Cormac looked from Brian to Astrid. His blue eyes pierced straight through her.

"They're gone," she choked.

"Who?" The word left his lips like a thunderclap.

"Duncan and Gormla," Brian supplied. "They can't be found."

Sitric stepped forward, joining the conversation. "Perhaps she took him to see the ships at the harbor—"

"Cahill and Teague are gone," Astrid interrupted. "Mother isn't at fault, Sitric. She's in danger."

Cormac motioned to the Fianna, drawing them over to join the conversation. Brian called his guards to him while Cormac explained the situation to the Fianna.

Astrid paced, her mind racing and her hands clenching in frustration. She felt so helpless. What could she possibly do?

"Find your weapons and bring my horse," Brian ordered the guards.

"Lord," Cormac protested.

Brian held a hand out, silencing him. "I will never be too old to protect my children."

Astrid's attention snapped to the aged king. She hated Brian for subjugating her brother, for taking Duncan from her mother, for sacking Dyflin. For so many things.

She would never love him. She probably wouldn't even like him, no matter how much she grew to know him.

But in that moment, Astrid respected him.

"Guards!" Sitric called. His men came over as well, the dueling square now filled with warriors. "Who was watching the gates?"

The men looked from one to another, a few shuffling their feet.

"Well?" Sitric demanded.

Harald, his captain, stepped forward. "I believe the men were all watching the duel."

Her brother's nostrils flared dangerously, his eyes blazing. Astrid would wager someone was going to be whipped for abandoning their post.

"The gate's open!" another of his men called from the front of the estate.

"She was going to take him to the harbor," Astrid told them. "I heard her talk of ships."

"Then that's where we go," Brian declared, turning his horse and taking off for the gates.

The Fianna rode ahead at a full gallop. The rest of Brian's and Sitric's men followed their kings on foot. Astrid joined them, desperate to help her mother and step-brother however she could. The rows of buildings and curious townsfolk turned to a blur in her haste to reach the harbor.

She smelled it before she saw it, the acrid, citrusy scent of pine and pitch mixing with the briny smell of the sea. The sounds came next: the shrieking cries of gulls, the clanking of boards and hammering of nails, orders being shouted from a dozen ships as they made berth in the largest port on this side of Éire. Masts and sails bobbed above the rooftops of the city, drawing Astrid like a beacon toward Dyflin's teeming shores.

Every sailor and craftsman in sight stood still when they entered the harbor with so great a number of warriors. Upon seeing Sitric and Astrid, most went back to their work with only a few curious glances as their party swept up and down the shoreline in search of Gormla and Duncan.

"Ratner!" Astrid called out to one of the captains who frequented the port. "Have you seen my mother?"

Ratner, a tall, thin man with a balding pate, pointed south. "She passed by a while ago with a young lad, looking at all the ships."

Astrid thanked him, following the herd of warriors who now rushed southward through the harbor. They found her shortly after that.

Gagged and tied to a large piece of driftwood, she sat alone, hidden behind a large boulder. Sitric pulled the gag from her mouth while his men cut her bonds.

"He took him!" she screeched. "Cahill took him! I tried to stop him, and Duncan fought them so well," her words grew more frantic as she went, her composure dissolving.

"Where did they go?" Brian demanded sharply.

Her mother's sky-blue eyes snapped to the king. "They're up there." She pointed even further south, to the white-faced cliffs that guarded the shore.

Sure enough, figures were visible even from this distance, moving about on top of them.

"He wants your oath, Brian," Gormla hissed. "And you'd better bring me back my son."

"What will you do?" Sitric asked. "Will you swear to Malachy for my brother's life? For your son's life?"

A debate broke out between the three of them, but it faded into the back of her thoughts as Astrid groped for a plan. Brian would never swear. She knew it, and she could hardly blame him for it, either. She despised the man, yes, but he'd risked everything to get to this point in his life, so close to uniting the kingdoms under his rule. He wasn't cruel, but he was pragmatic, and Astrid knew he'd do everything in his power to avoid swearing to Malachy.

Her eyes scanned the harbor, from the cliff where her half-brother was being held hostage to the far northern horizon filled with masts and sails. The wind blew hard, whipping the sails against their ropes, the ships swaying in their berths.

And then it hit her.

Striding in between her bickering family, Astrid hushed them all. "I have an idea," she announced. "But it's risky."

CHAPTER THIRTY

"R ISKY" DID NOT begin to cover the incredible danger of Astrid's plan. Bold and clever, aye. But so many things could go wrong, and all of them put lives at risk—Duncan's in particular.

The despair of his last conversation with Astrid yet crushed him, but Cormac pushed it out of his mind. He knew she could never forgive him for battling Sitric. Even if she did, there would always be a rift between them—his oath to Brian. No matter how much she loved him, he didn't expect her to betray her family any more than he could his. Fate, it seemed, conspired against them at every turn.

Cormac's mind raced as he urged his horse up the steep hill to the top of the cliff. They needed to get to Cahill with all speed so that Astrid had enough time to enact her plan without him noticing.

They were the distraction.

The Fianna arrived first, as planned, to draw Cahill's attention away from the harbor while Brian and his guards made their way up to bargain with Cahill.

It was the same promontory where Astrid took him to watch the Northern Lights dance across the sky—a memory he held dear in spite of its bittersweet ending. The cloudy afternoon cast a grey pall over the clifftop, the trampled grass and littering of stones and bare earth as gloomy as Cormac's mood.

Cahill's men stood nearest, forming a line to protect Cahill,

Teague, and Duncan, who perched far too close to the cliff's rugged edge. It was a steep fall, but not so high that the distance alone might kill a man. The rocks that jutted out along the cliff and those hidden beneath the sea, however, were deadly.

"You're not a villain," Cormac called to his father. "You won't kill a boy."

The Fianna dismounted, standing shoulder-to-shoulder in a line that faced Cahill's men. It would be an easy fight—hardly a battle—but it put Duncan's life at too great a risk to simply attack. Cormac wanted to believe that whatever their disagreement, his father wouldn't actually harm young Duncan, but it wasn't a risk he was prepared to take. That trust had been shattered the day Cahill turned his back on his children.

"Hostages are a part of war," Cahill called back. "As are casualties."

Cormac didn't much care for that answer. "What game do you play, then? Hostages always serve a purpose."

"All I require is Brian's oath of loyalty to Malachy and a guarantee of peace. Where is he?"

"He's on his way." Cormac couldn't let Cahill turn behind him, else he'd see Astrid and Sitric hard at work, ruining their plan. It all hinged on the element of surprise. If they lost that, they may lose Duncan.

"Is this why you came?" Cormac shouted angrily. "To capture a boy?"

"I came to ally with Sitric," Cahill spat, "but that proved a fruitless endeavor. The boy is the next best option. Better, even, if it stops all this battling."

"You could stop fighting, you know," Conan growled. "You invade Mumhain as often as we retaliate."

Hoofs sounded behind them as Brian and his guards appeared behind the Fianna. Brian's eyes blazed in fury as he took in the sight before him.

"Give me my son, Cahill," he demanded.

"I could say the same thrice over," Cahill shot back. "You

stole three of my sons and my only daughter. It seems fitting I should take one of your children."

"You abandoned us!" Cormac knew he should stay silent and let Brian negotiate, but his heart hammered in outrage. "You disowned us—your own children. You cast us aside without even the courtesy of a conversation."

"I told you to come with me. You refused. I left." Cahill shrugged. "What would you have had me do?"

"We were still of fostering age, and I'd spent the past seven years with Brian. Of course I would choose to stay. I hardly remembered life in Connachta."

"You wish you'd chosen differently then, boy? Is that it?" Cahill smirked. "Swear your oath to Malachy and I will take you back."

Cormac's fists clenched at his sides. Why had he wasted so many years angry with this man? Swallowing his anger, he shook his head, feeling so much like the boy he'd been that night so long ago.

"No, you're right," he managed. "There's no sense in anger unless I would change the outcome." He looked his father dead in the eyes. "And I would not."

A weight lifted from Cormac, his breath light in his chest. He'd made the right choice then, even though he'd been so young. And he'd make it again every chance he got. He needn't feel guilty over robbing his brothers of a father. He should be proud that he found them a better one.

"Enough of this," Cahill snarled. "Brian, you must make your decision. Will you take your oath or will you take your son's life?"

Brian hesitated, and for good reason. They'd stalled nearly as long as they could, but Astrid had yet to give the signal that they were ready. If the sails weren't in place, he and Duncan would hit the rocks when they went over the edge.

"What is your plan?" Cormac called, trying to bait his father and distract him longer. "Whatever happens, you're surrounded and you've threatened the life of the Prince of Mumhain. How do you imagine this will end?"

Cahill narrowed his eyes, but held his tongue.

"Brian," Cahill hissed, "this is between you and me. Answer me. Your oath or your son. No more of this nonsense."

"Let us duel," Conan offered. "You may choose any of us to fight any of your men. We'll solve it without endangering a boy."

Cormac allowed himself a small smile when Duncan rolled his eyes, scowling. He *hated* being called a child, and apparently his life being threatened didn't change his reaction to it. His smile lasted only a moment, though, for his worries far outshadowed his amusement.

Astrid still hadn't given the signal.

And they were just about out of time.

"Something's going on here," Cahill grumbled. He took a step backward.

One of Brian's guards gasped behind them.

Cahill glanced over the cliff's edge, and Cormac knew it was over. A catlike grin spread across his father's face as he walked farther from the edge. "I see," he cooed. "You thought I would push him, did you?"

The blood rushed through Cormac's ears, a pulsing whoosh that blocked out all thought. He watched as Cahill motioned Teague over.

As Teague pulled his dagger.

And hesitated.

Cormac did the only thing he could—he charged. He reached Duncan a moment before Teague, who grabbed hold of Cormac to try to stop him. But Cormac wasn't trying to steal Duncan. Instead of battling Teague, Cormac kept running until he no longer felt the earth beneath his feet, holding Duncan to his chest as they fell from the cliff.

CHAPTER THIRTY-ONE

THEY NEARLY HAD it. They'd needed more ropes than they thought, and those had been a devil to attach to the rocks without causing them to fall. With a few well-placed knots and several of their strongest men there to act as leverage, almost eighty feet of good woolen sailcloth would provide a safe landing from the cliff. Two corners were stretched across the cliff. Two more were tethered to longships sailing out to pull the cloth flat. When they were in place, Astrid could give the signal.

She watched from the shore, bow nocked and waiting for the last men to take position. She'd already considered simply shooting Cahill, but unfortunately her shortbow didn't have the range to make the shot safely. Otherwise, she'd not have hesitated. No one threatened her brother and left with his life.

The longships cut across the choppy sea, the oars bringing the ships to life as they forded wave after crashing wave. They were so close.

A scream tore through the silence. A heartwrenching cry.

Astrid looked up to see three men falling from the cliff— Teague, Duncan, and Cormac. Too early. They were too early.

"Row!" Astrid screamed at the oarsmen. "Row!"

She knew it was no use. She knew they wouldn't make it, for the sea fought their every stroke.

The men hit the sails in a mess of limbs and glittering weapons. And the sails held.

Astrid let out a breath, rushing down the length of the beach to follow the men's progress. They hadn't broken through the sails, but that was the only good news. The ships weren't in position, and the men rolled down the loose cloths and into the raging sea.

She couldn't see them. Had they hit any of the rocks hidden beneath the surface? Were the ships able to get them aboard? A thousand worries flooded her as she searched for any signs of the men. Between the sails and the ships and the rocks, Astrid couldn't see a thing.

She heard another yell and a splash, but it must have been on the far side of the cliff and out of her sight completely.

Commotion broke out on the ships. She saw men running across the deck on the nearest one. The rowers stopped. They must be taking the men aboard. They must be.

The longship turned toward the shore, but she couldn't see. She cursed aloud. Why could she not see them? Were they alright?

Astrid counted every second until they reached shore. Six hundred. She counted to six hundred as the longship sailed down the shore and back to its berth. Astrid ran alongside it, unable to stand still as she waited for the men to disembark.

The air left her lungs in a rush when Cormac jumped from the ship into the shallows. Teague followed behind, and together they helped Duncan down.

Her mother shot from behind her with a cry, not stopping until she pulled Duncan into a smothering hug and started checking him for injuries. Cormac also looked over the lad, his face contorted in concern.

Astrid watched them, fighting to breathe. He was alive. He was okay, and so was Duncan. She hadn't gotten them killed.

Cormac ruffled Duncan's sopping hair affectionately, then looked toward the shore. She knew the moment he saw her, their gazes locking, his whole body going still. Astrid was done waiting.

She ran across the sandy shore, ignoring the icy bite of the water that seeped into her shoes. His arms opened and she threw herself into them. He was soaking wet. His hair dripped. Every inch of her came into contact with water in his embrace.

And she couldn't have cared less.

Grabbing his face with her hands, she pulled him into a kiss—hard and deep and filled with all the longing she felt. His tongue parted her lips, roughly demanding, taking. He was her whole world. He was the place where she wanted to be.

She pulled back, her hands frantically searching him for injuries.

Cormac's hands grasped hers, engulfing them in warmth. His stormy blue eyes, the same color as the raging sea beyond, stared into her very soul. "What of Brian?" he asked, his voice rough. "What of our divided loyalties? What of leaving your people, your home?"

Squeezing his hands, she swallowed, searching for the right words. "You've taught me something over these past weeks," she whispered. "Home isn't a place. It's a person. And my home is you."

His hand caressed her face. "Astrid, I love you."

Her heart swelled so that she thought it might burst. "I love you, too."

"That's terribly romantic, but he needs to get a change of clothes or he won't live to the wedding," Gormla called as she walked past them.

"Thank you both," Duncan said, following right behind her. "Did you have to call me 'boy' so much, though? Honestly, Cormac, it's insulting. I'm old enough to marry."

"I was trying to make him feel worse about it," Cormac defended. "Fight your first battle, and I'll stop calling you 'boy.' Most of the time," he grinned.

Teague followed behind them, and Astrid's fury returned with a vengeance. She jumped for him, prepared to break his nose or anything else she could reach.

"How dare you, you son of a whore!" she cried as her fist connected with his cheek. "How dare you!"

"Whoa, Astrid! Hold on," Cormac's hands encircled her waist, pulling her off Teague.

"What are you doing?" she cried. "He deserves a sound thrashing. Maybe even an execution!"

"I spoke with him," Cormac explained softly. "He's helping us now, but from the inside."

"What?" Astrid shot a disgusted look at Teague. "Like a spy?"

"Precisely," Teague replied. "I agreed with my father's idea of an alliance. But I wanted no part in kidnapping your brother."

"And yet you were there," Astrid sniped.

"I was." Teague swallowed hard. "And for that I am sorry. My thinking was that it was better to go along with it so that at least one of the boy's captors was prepared to keep him from dying. I would not have killed him."

Astrid didn't know if she believed him, but Cormac appeared to trust him. "We'll see," she allowed. "What of your father?" She looked toward the cliff, realizing that whatever had transpired up there must be finished by now. "What was his plan of escape?"

"He honestly thought Brian would swear the oath to save Duncan and then let him leave."

"Then he's more a fool than I gave him credit for," Cormac frowned.

"You understand I cannot return with you," Teague said. "I must find my father's men and play the part. We will return to Connachta as soon as possible. I wish you a long and happy marriage."

Cormac nodded to him, then followed Astrid out of the harbor. They needed to learn what happened after Cormac jumped. Near the entrance to Sitric's holding, Astrid and Cormac crossed paths with Brian and the Fianna.

Astrid searched the crowd of warriors, but couldn't find Cahill among them. "What happened to him?" she asked. "Where is he?"

"He jumped," Brian told her. "He didn't miss the rocks. I'm sorry, Cormac. He wasn't a good man, but he was your father."

"He was no father to me," Cormac replied. "Not as you were."

Brian dismounted to embrace Cormac. "Come," he spoke to everyone, "we have a wedding to attend."

Cormac took Astrid's hand, a wicked grin on his handsome face as he led her back up the hill.

CHAPTER THIRTY-TWO

THE FOLLOWING NIGHT Sitric hosted a wedding feast that Cormac would remember for the rest of his life. He and Astrid were to be wed in the Ostman tradition, as it was important to her and he didn't have strong feelings on the manner of the marriage. In truth, he'd never attended an Ostman ceremony and was excited at the idea.

The tables in the hall were laden with the most decadent feast Cormac had seen yet: roast ox, buttered carrots, honeyed salmon, a hearty stew, fresh oat bread, and a dessert made of spiced apple preserves and ground hazelnuts. And, of course, enough mead, ale, and wine to drown them all.

He stood with Astrid in the center of the hall, holding her hands before the roaring hearthfire, and wondering how he could be so lucky. Conan stood behind him as his groomsman. Eva took up the post of bridesmaid beside Astrid.

And Astrid stole the breath from his lungs.

She wore an apron tunic of brightest blue, hung with strands of gems in every color. On her arms were golden bands she'd earned throughout her life, most gifted to her by her brother, he later learned. And on her face she wore the smile that had captivated him from the start.

They swore their oaths to one another, invoking the goddess Vár, who safeguards the oaths between men and women. Finn, Dallan, and his brothers all worked with him to write an oath appropriate to the ceremony, though it still took all his effort not to let his nerves get the better of him.

Once they were oathsworn, Conan passed him a ring of brass keys to gift her and a delicate golden armband he'd bought for her. She tied the keys to her belt, then took off all her other armbands. Cormac slid the gift over her slender wrist and up past her elbow until it fit snugly.

Astrid took a similar golden armband from Eva, placing it on Cormac's arm in return.

"Kiss her!" Someone shouted from the men's table. Cormac guessed it was Diarmid, but couldn't be sure. He had trouble taking his eyes off his wife.

The rest of their guests clamored in agreement to the suggestion, which worked just fine for Cormac. He planned to kiss his wife as often as possible, and this seemed as good a time as ever to start.

Unable to keep a grin off his face, he kissed her until they were both laughing, until the cheers of the crowd faded into the distance.

Until she knew, without a doubt, that she was home.

THE NEXT WEEKS were bliss. Astrid and Cormac stayed in Dyflin for a fortnight following the wedding so that they could spend time together before Cormac had to leave on another mission for Brian. Sitric gave them use of one of the guest houses, and Astrid was happy to spend most of their days in there working toward those children she'd always wanted.

When they left, they went to Cenn Cora, the Fianna's fortress in the far west of Mumhain. Astrid hadn't realized that they didn't live in Caiseal, and she was pleased when Cormac told her Cenn Cora was near to Luimneach—a settlement with many Ostmen, much like Dyflin.

The fortress at Cenn Cora sat upon a wooded hillside, with a sleepy lake hugging the valley below. Though they were an hour's ride from the sea, the presence of a large lake comforted Astrid. Patchwork farm fields and a smattering of cottages dotted the surrounding countryside. She hadn't imagined a place could be so peaceful.

They rode up the hill and through the palisade to the courtyard, stuffed to bursting with well-wishers waiting to greet them. Eva and Finn. Niamh and Dallan. Cara and Diarmid. Conan pulled them into a warm hug as well, followed closely by Illadan.

"I don't believe you've met my wife, Ethlinn," he said, gesturing to a tall, beautiful brunette standing beside him. "She's Finn's sister."

"And our daughter." A woman of a size with Ethlinn stepped forward, smiling. She was older, with greying braids falling about her shoulders, delicate features, and sharp gaze.

"We hear you come from Dyflin." A man taller than most of the Fianna stepped up beside the woman, with a grey beard and a wild smile. "I'm Ulf Thorsson. This is my wife, Elan."

It took Astrid a moment to realize he'd spoken in *Norrøna*. She knew that Finn's father was an Ostman, but she hadn't expected to move somewhere with so many of her kinsmen, and so many folk who spoke the language besides. Something embarrassingly close to tears formed in the corners of her eyes.

Beside her, Cormac squeezed her hand. "They have kin in Luimneach," he told her, also speaking the language. His grasp of it had grown much in the weeks since he began learning.

"My brother would love to meet an Ostman princess," Ulf said cheerily. "Arne travels much and has many tales to tell. We will visit him when the men leave again."

"I would like that very much," she replied in the same tongue, fighting those damned tears. "Thank you."

As Cormac led Astrid to their quarters in the keep, she couldn't help but marvel at the irony of it all. She'd married a Gael. She'd moved to the heart of Éire.

And somehow, she'd ended up exactly where she belonged.

ABOUT THE AUTHOR

Sophia has been telling stories since she could talk. She loves learning almost as much as she loves writing, pursuing both her undergraduate and master's degrees. She has studied archaeology, anthropology, and the languages and histories of a variety of cultures. Her master's degree is in medieval history, with a focus on the British Isles. She's been fortunate enough to participate in three archaeological excavations and surveys–one at a Native American settlement in southern Indiana, one at a Tudor estate in Essex, and one at an early medieval ringfort in County Roscommon, Ireland.

After marrying her high school sweetheart, attending grad school, and moving nearly ten times in as many years, Sophia and her husband settled into a lake house in northern Indiana. When she isn't working on her next novel, you can find her in the garden and covered in dirt. They live happily in the middle of nowhere with two little boys, two atrociously rude doggos, and one ornery cat.

Facebook:
facebook.com/SophiaNyeWrites

Instagram:
instagram.com/sophianyewrites

TikTok:
tiktok.com/@sophianyewrites

BookBub:
bookbub.com/authors/sophia-nye

Goodreads:
goodreads.com/author/show/20815931.Sophia_Nye

Amazon Author Page:
amazon.com/Sophia-Nye/e/B08L9XZ148

Website:
sophianyewrites.com

www.ingramcontent.com/pod-product-compliance
Lightning Source LLC
Chambersburg PA
CBHW072131300726

48975CB00003B/1010